Adachi and Shimamura

STORY BY **Hitoma Iruma** ART BY **Non**

NOVEL **8**

Shimamura

A girl with a bit of a ditzy side. As the school trip approaches, she's still not sure how to handle her new romantic relationship with Adachi.

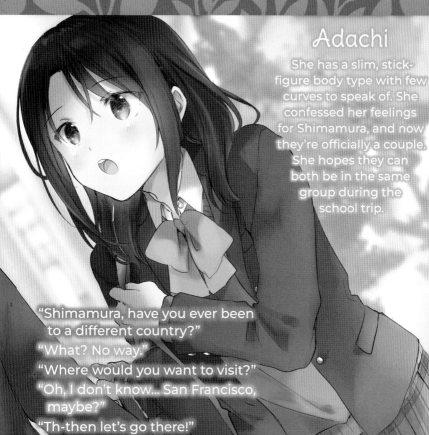

Adachi

She has a slim, stick-figure body type with few curves to speak of. She confessed her feelings for Shimamura, and now they're officially a couple. She hopes they can both be in the same group during the school trip.

"Shimamura, have you ever been to a different country?"

"What? No way."

"Where would you want to visit?"

"Oh, I don't know... San Francisco, maybe?"

"Th-then let's go there!"

"Go where?"

"San Fran!"

"When exactly are we going? Right now?"

"Uh...i-if you want to!"

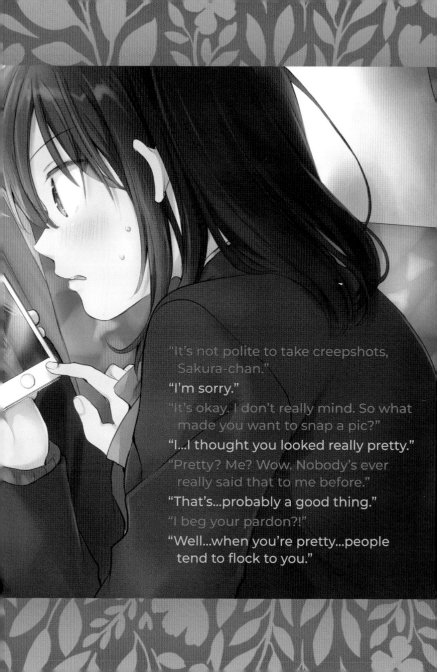

"It's not polite to take creepshots, Sakura-chan."

"I'm sorry."

"It's okay. I don't really mind. So what made you want to snap a pic?"

"I...I thought you looked really pretty."

"Pretty? Me? Wow. Nobody's ever really said that to me before."

"That's...probably a good thing."

"I beg your pardon?!"

"Well...when you're pretty...people tend to flock to you."

Table of Contents

ADACHI TO SHIMAMURA VOL. 8

© Hitoma Iruma 2019
Edited by Dengeki Bunko
Illustrations by Non

First published in Japan in 2019 by
KADOKAWA CORPORATION, Tokyo.
English translation rights arranged with
KADOKAWA CORPORATION, Tokyo.

Seven Seas press and purchase enquiries can be sent to
Marketing Manager Lianne Sentar at press@gomanga.com.
Information regarding the distribution and purchase of
digital editions is available from Digital Manager CK Russell
at digital@gomanga.com.

Follow Seven Seas Entertainment online at
sevenseasentertainment.com.

TRANSLATION: Molly Lee
COVER DESIGN: Nicky Lim
LOGO DESIGN: George Panella
INTERIOR LAYOUT & DESIGN: Clay Gardner
COPY EDITOR: Meg van Huygen
LIGHT NOVEL EDITOR: Nibedita Sen
PREPRESS TECHNICIAN: Melanie Ujimori
PRINT MANAGER: Rhiannon Rasmussen-Silverstein
PRODUCTION MANAGER: Lissa Pattillo
MANAGING EDITOR: Julie Davis
ASSOCIATE PUBLISHER: Adam Arnold
PUBLISHER: Jason DeAngelis

ISBN: 978-1-64827-276-9
Printed in Canada
First Printing: February 2022
10 9 8 7 6 5 4 3 2 1

Adachi and Shimamura

NOVEL

STORY BY

Hitoma Iruma

ILLUSTRATED BY

Non

Seven Seas Entertainment

1. Setting Off

"**W**HENEVER I GO VISIT my parents, they always wanna talk about the past, you know?"

"Yeah?"

"I didn't get it at first, but after I thought about it, I realized it actually makes a lot of sense. Like, in terms of their age, their past is a lot longer than their future, so yeah. No wonder they're always talking about old memories."

"Right..."

"Maybe we'll end up reminiscing all the time, too. What do you think, Adachi?"

"Hmmm..." She paused to think for a moment. "That might be nice."

"Right?"

This was the conversation we had as I packed my suitcase. As for Adachi, she said she wasn't going to pack until later tonight; for now, she was sitting on the sofa, watching TV. Onscreen, I could see some sort of educational program, with a child in a familiar-looking spacesuit wiggling idly as a man in a white lab coat gave a lecture about something. But if I had to guess, Adachi wasn't really paying attention.

The faint heat of May drifted in through the open window. Compared to summer in full swing, the humidity wasn't quite as oppressive. This was probably how I felt the last time May rolled around too. But that suited me just fine. If my opinion of the seasons changed with every single year, I'd probably wear myself out before long.

Together, the two of us had picked out an apartment and moved in. We went shopping together, used the same household supplies, slept in the same bed, and breathed the same air. Everything in the house was just enough for two. This was the year Adachi and I turned 27—and at least for now, the future ahead still felt longer than my past.

After checking the contents one last time, it was time to zip my suitcase shut...*shut*...SHUT! I leaned my body weight down onto it to force it closed. If I unzipped it even a little, it was liable to spring open like a jack-in-the-box, so hopefully, I wouldn't need to open it until we made it to the hotel. Briefly, I contemplated whether to slap a post-it note on the front so I wouldn't forget.

Tomorrow marked the start of our big trip overseas. For the first time in my life, I was going to leave Japan—partly to keep a promise, partly as a celebration, partly as a reward for working hard, but mostly to step outside my comfort zone. In other words, this trip held a lot of significance for me. A deep sense of sentimentality flooded my chest.

"How long's it been since the last time we went on a trip, anyway?"

"Um...since high school?" As far as I could remember, anyway. If I was right, then it had been eight or nine years—eh, roughly ten years, let's say. Nearly the same length of time that I'd known Adachi.

"Oh, yeah, the school trip... That brings back a lot of memories," she murmured.

"Do you even remember what we did on that trip?"

"Nope."

"Correct me if I'm wrong, but didn't you just say it *brings back memories*?"

She didn't respond. Normally, I would have stormed over there and pinched her ear or her cheek or whatever I could get my hands on, but right now I was busy packing my *other* bag. Unlike her, I didn't have time to sit around and wait for tomorrow. I had promised my parents I would visit at some point during Golden Week, and since we were using the rest of it for the trip, today was the only time I had available. Hence, I was scrambling back and forth.

As previously mentioned, I didn't generally do a lot of traveling, so I kept belatedly remembering things and stuffing them into my carry-on. Then I'd realize they weren't essential and take them out again...but then I'd remember something *else*, and the cycle would continue. It wasn't fun, to say the least.

"So you're not gonna go see your mom before we go?" I asked.

"Meh... No need."

She changed the channel to something about a deserted island. Then it started talking about these little birds I'd seen before in the mountains nearby, and that was when I finally learned what they were called. From now on, perhaps I would make a conscious effort to look up at the birds whenever I went for a walk. For me, learning was always a good thing. It was only after I learned Adachi's name that she rose to the forefront of the nebulous category labeled "classmates."

She had yet to visit her parents' house a single time since the day she moved in with me, but...given their strained relationship, maybe it was for the best. To me, it was sad, but in this case, the only opinion that really mattered was Adachi's.

Becoming a legal adult didn't magically solve anything. In fact, it only made me feel like *more* of a screw-up for constantly putting my problems on the backburner. Every now and then I thought to myself: *With age comes wisdom, and wisdom is a curse.*

Slinging my backpack over my shoulder, I walked to the fridge and opened it, just to check. We were planning to be gone for quite a while, so we'd emptied it as best we could. Thinking back to the ketchup *udon* stir-fry that Adachi threw together last night, I closed the door. A pleasant gust of chilled air brushed past the left half of my face.

All we had to drink was the water from the thermos I'd refrigerated in advance. I never could get used to this stuff. Unlike the well water at my parents' house, the city water smelled of fluoride.

Once my suitcase and backpack were finally ready to go, I hurried to the front door; Adachi heard my footsteps and got up from the sofa to see me off. Her hair was longer now than when we were teenagers, which made her look all the more adult, and her previously aloof attitude had softened considerably in the time since then. Sometimes I liked to reminisce about that panicky passion she used to have, but...frankly, with a little teasing, I could see it again anytime I wanted.

"Well, I'll see you at the airport."

"Okay."

Once I left, I wasn't coming back here until after the trip was over. "Pretty exciting, don't you think?"

"Is it?" she blinked, tilting her head in mild puzzlement. At some point our roles had reversed, and now *she* was the calm, rational one—at least, on the outside. "Personally, I don't like anything that gets in the way of us spending time together."

"...Hm."

"But it's just one measly day apart. I have faith that our trip together will more than make up for it."

"...Hmmm..."

Gah, so cheesy! I tried to play it off, but on the inside I was squirming bashfully. Then, as the seconds passed,

Adachi started to boil until her ears were as pink as the flowers she was named after. *Ah, just like the good old days.* For a split second, she had gone back to the faltering teenager I once knew.

"Come on, Shimamura, now it's your turn to say something cringey."

She had hoisted herself with her own petard, and now she was trying to hoist *me*.

"...Gosh, how can I possibly choose?"

"You have a lot?"

She looked at me in surprise. Naturally, I was bluffing. My gaze darted to and fro until finally, mercifully, I thought of something.

"The other day, I accidentally wore your underwear to work." I'd slept through my alarm, and as I rushed to get dressed, I didn't take a close look at what I was pulling on.

Adachi froze. Then, belatedly, she repeated: "To work?"

"Yeah."

She didn't really react to this. "And that's...cringey?"

"Well, it was for me!"

At first, I was sincerely confused as to whose panties I was wearing. Then it hit me: I recognized them from the laundry hamper. *Such* a relief. When I got home that day, I snuck them into the dirty laundry and vowed never to let Adachi find out...and yet here I was, confessing my secret. Not that she seemed to care.

But after a long moment, she finally chuckled. "I swear, you have no class."

"Say wha?!" Sometimes, it really felt like she could read my mind.

After this somewhat long goodbye, I started heading out for real.

"Well, see you tomorrow."

"Okay."

This exchange wasn't much different from the one we had earlier, but we went through the motions regardless. Honestly, I loved making overly optimistic promises with her. It was so much fun to plan for the future with someone else.

As I opened the door, a voice called out hastily from behind me: "What pattern—er, what color were they? The panties?" For some reason, Adachi was as stiff as a board.

"Dare I ask why you want to know...?"

Starting tomorrow, we were embarking on our first-ever international adventure. If I said I wasn't excited, I'd be a total liar.

When I arrived at my parents' house, I was baffled to find that the front door was unlocked. *You're getting lazy, Mom,* I sighed silently to myself. I started to ring the doorbell, but as my finger hovered uselessly in midair, yet another lazybones arrived. It was a little shark, holding a rice ball and walking on two legs.

"I had a feeling it was you, Shimamura-san," she called with a grin over the pitter-patter of her little feet. "Welcome home."

"Great to be back."

It was Yashiro, welcoming me into my parents' house like she was part of the family. For fun, I picked her up and lifted her into the air. She weighed practically nothing.

"Wheeee!" She swung her arms and legs in sheer delight.

Over the past decade, absolutely nothing had changed about her. Her height, her hair, her bright smile—they were all just as I remembered. The one difference was that she had gone from lion PJs to shark PJs. Now she was both the king of the jungle *and* the ruler of the seas...but in both cases, her head always wound up in an animal's mouth.

"It's been so long!" she exclaimed.

"No, it hasn't," I corrected her. After all, we just saw each other two days ago. Every now and then, she would show up at my apartment out of nowhere, eat my food, and leave. By this point, Adachi had gotten used to having her around, and on rare occasions, I would even catch a glimpse of her sneaking Yashiro a treat.

But my apartment was a considerable distance from my parents' house, so I was amazed she could make the trip without breaking a sweat. She seemed to defy every law of physics, time, and space. In a sense, I envied that about her...assuming there were no downsides, of course.

"What's with the rice ball?"

"It is my snack. It contains kelp," she informed me, not that I really needed to know. "Would you care for a bite?"

"Hmmm... Okay, maybe just a bite." I opened my mouth wide.

"Remember, you only get *one bite*."

"I know, I know."

I nibbled one corner. It tasted exactly like the salted rice balls my mother would always make for me to take to field day at school. Not sure about junior high, but when I was back in elementary school, I eagerly took part in all the school events. I could still feel the lingering traces of that passion like a scar on my skin.

Then Yashiro ate the rest of her rice ball in a single bite. For a little kid, her mouth was *huge*. "This large rice ball has filled 10 percent of my hunger meter!"

"That's practically nothing!" I couldn't imagine what it would be like to get hungry again after a hundred steps. "So what's the story behind those pajamas, anyway?"

"They were a gift from Little." She flapped her fins.

"You've got some weird taste, sis..." Looking back, my little sister always did love to take care of aquatic animals. Not that she ever owned a shark.

I lowered Yashiro to the floor and readjusted my backpack straps; she slurped the stray grains of rice from her fingers, then ran off. So I followed that tiny beacon all the way to the living room, where I found the aforementioned sister lounging in front of the TV with her legs splayed. She looked up at the sound of Yashiro's footsteps, then looked at me without even batting a lash. "Oh, hey, you're here."

"Just got here, yeah."

"I was wondering where Yachi ran off to. Thought maybe she went to get some candy."

She spread her arms wide, inviting Yashiro to join her. Sure enough, the little girl ran up and settled between my sister's legs. She was then given an animal cookie, as if in greeting; it made a pleasant crunch as she bit down. Surely, a shark wouldn't eat something as cute and fanciful as *animal cookies*.

But now I had to wonder: How did Yashiro sense that I was at the door if I never rang the doorbell? It was reminiscent of the way a dog or cat would randomly stare into empty space.

"Where's Mom?"

"Kitchen."

If I listened closely, I could hear the sound of a kitchen knife tapping against a cutting board.

I set my luggage in the corner, then sat down a short distance away from my sister, behind her and to the side. From behind, she reminded me of me when I was her age, particularly the long hair and the posture. Of course, I'd never actually observed myself from behind, so I couldn't say for sure, but still. It was weird.

I was kinda hoping you wouldn't turn out like me, but oh, well. The cue ball of fate had sent me flying and nudged her into my place instead.

Her fingers curled around Yashiro's shark hood and pulled it down, revealing her sky-blue hair in a torrent of sparkles. Smiling, my sister stroked the girl's head, her pale fingers cresting the waves like white foam. Meanwhile, she periodically brought a cookie to Yashiro's mouth, and Yashiro was more than happy to oblige. These days there was a significant height difference between them, but their friendship hadn't changed one bit. If anything, they seemed closer than ever.

"Don't spoil her too much, now," I cautioned her, even though I knew this warning was ten years too late. But my sister shrugged it off.

"What do you mean? Look at her. She's so cute! Right, Yachi?" She peeked at the little girl's face.

Yashiro blinked back, mouth full of cookie. "I beg your pardon?" she asked, her eyes round and innocent. To this day, the two of them really seemed like siblings, even as the gap in their ages continued to widen every year.

"Besides, Mom spoils her a lot too."

"I guess when you're that cute, you get everything handed to you..."

Upon further consideration, maybe it wasn't much different from owning a cat or dog. Especially dogs. So dang cute.

"The neighbors all think she's an international exchange student."

"What, from overseas?"

"Yes, I come from over the sea! Ha ha ha!" Yashiro

declared thoughtlessly. *A sea of* stars, *maybe*. As she crunched on a frog-shaped cookie, her molars glittered pale blue like her eyes. *You, my dear, are a creature beyond mortal comprehension.*

"Over the sea, hm...?"

Tomorrow, I too would travel to the other side of the ocean. What would it feel like? Like being teleported to the other side of a TV screen? The longer I thought about it, the fuzzier I felt. Were there more of Yashiro's kind waiting for me over there?

"Would it kill you to let me know you're here?"

Just then, someone flicked my head. When I tried to turn and look, she did it again. Then she started tapping on my skull over and over until finally it pissed me off so much, I whirled around aggressively. There stood my mother, stooped over slightly and tormenting me with both hands. She froze for a moment, then started smacking my forehead next.

"Hey!"

I slapped her hands away. She promptly stopped and straightened her posture. The earthy smell of onions wafted to my nose.

"Now, what do you say?" she demanded, palm up. Her entitled attitude did *not* encourage me to cooperate. But

I couldn't think of a good comeback, so in the end, I was left with no other choice.

"I'm back, Mom."

"Good. Welcome home. If you had any common sense, this is the first thing you'd think to do when you got here! You really ought to learn some manners."

"I was just about to come find you, okay?"

"Keh!"

She stormed off back to the kitchen. If anyone was rude here, it was *her*. But, setting her bratty behavior aside, I *was* technically supposed to let her know I made it here safe.

"You really haven't improved at all, have you, Nee-chan?"

All my life, my little sister would always point and laugh whenever I got in trouble. In the past I would have punished her for it, but now that I was sitting down, it would take *way* too much effort to get up again. That's how I knew I was officially an adult. At some point, I had lost the energy needed to chase her down.

"Okay, no more cookies for today." She gave one more to Yashiro, who crunched it into dust within seconds. "When I was in high school, I must've spent at least a third of my allowance on snacks for Yachi," she continued wistfully. "But hey. Sometimes, money *can* buy happiness. And when you can get it for cheap, that's a bargain."

She tugged Yashiro's cheeks, and they stretched like *mochi* as the girl in question grinned. Both of them seemed so content.

"Yeah, that makes sense."

I could see where she was coming from. In the same vein, I spent my hard-earned cash to put a smile on Adachi's face.

For dinner we had okonomiyaki, tamagoyaki, and yakisoba.

"That's a lot of *yaki*."

"You like these things, right?"

"Well, yeah..."

"I like them as well!" Yashiro volunteered, raising her hand gleefully. Personally, I'd be more interested to learn if there was anything she *didn't* like to eat.

She was sitting in the chair I used to sit in, next to my younger sister. Apparently, this was something of a routine for them. I sat in the vacant chair normally occupied by my father. "Where's Dad?"

"He went night fishing with the neighbor."

"He just can't get enough, huh?"

At some point over the years, my father had become *obsessed* with fishing. Sometimes, he'd walk down the hall yelling, "Gotta go fish!" so to be honest, I wasn't sure how he ever managed to catch anything.

All that aside, I had a newfound appreciation for my parents' house—a place where you could just sit around and food would magically appear on the table. *What a wonderful place to live*, I mused to myself as I chewed a bite of *okonomiyaki*. The sweet taste of cabbage and onions spread on my tongue…

Wait, what? I cocked my head in confusion. Experimentally, I cut another piece from the other side of the pancake, examined the cross-section, and popped it into my mouth. Sure enough, it tasted great and all, but…

"I, uh, notice there's no meat in this."

My mother chuckled coolly. "Heh, yeah! I thought we had some in the fridge, but we didn't."

Upon further inspection, I realized the yakisoba was just cabbage and noodles too.

"Relax. I already hit it with the Sauce Beam and Aonori Flash, so it's edible, trust me!" she insisted, shutting down the conversation before it could continue.

"This happens a lot," my sister shrugged as she quietly slurped her noodles.

"...Well, okay, then."

This was just part of the Shimamura family's cooking style...I guess.

Next, I took a bite of my omelet, the recipe for which thankfully didn't call for meat. The soft, sweet egg enveloped my molars and my heart. Now *this* was what I thought of when I thought about my mother's home cooking. But even then, I wasn't enjoying it *nearly* as much as the strange child who had been living here for the past ten years.

"Tastes like destiny!"

"You're a bigger brat than you let on, you know that?"

The longer I watched her, the more it felt like the plates and pots might come to life and start singing. But the happy little shark didn't even notice my gaze.

A few minutes after we finished eating, my sister rose from the table. "It's time to take a bath, Yachi," she announced as she took the little girl's hand in hers.

"That will not be necessary for today!"

"Oh, I'm afraid it's *very* necessary."

Before Yashiro could escape, my sister grabbed her by the scruff of the neck and carried her off. The captured shark flailed her fins, but alas, it was in vain—though if I had to guess, she wasn't seriously trying to escape in the first place. Just then, however, my sister looked over her shoulder...and while I knew it was something I couldn't possibly have seen before, it gave me an intense feeling of *déjà vu*, like I was watching a younger version of myself.

"I think I finally understand how you must have felt when you were dealing with me," she murmured wistfully.

"...Yeah?"

"Yeah. Now let's go, Yachi!"

And so my sister carried the wriggly shark all the way to the bathroom. Meanwhile, I ruminated on the concept of a sisterly bond.

"I wonder how it felt..."

When I paused to actually think about it, the lack of an immediate answer made me panic on the inside. But I couldn't exactly ask her to elaborate without looking like a loser fishing for compliments... As the TV droned in the background, my vision swirled with my thoughts. The things I always took for granted all blurred together in my memories.

"Hrrmm," said the only other person left in the room with me. I looked up to find my mother standing there.

"What is it?"

"So you're going on a trip?" she asked, like it was somehow news to her.

I stared at her in confusion. "Didn't I tell you about it over the phone the other day?"

"Yes, you did. And yes, I remember. Hah!" she scoffed, shrugging her shoulders.

As usual, I could never grasp where her snotty attitude came from. "Well? What about it?"

"Beats me." She was the one who started this conversation, and yet she tilted her head like she didn't have anything to say. "Well, whatever." Just like that, she single-handedly came to terms with whatever her issue was and walked off without me.

"What was *that* about...?"

My mother never made any sense, not just in terms of personality, but her appearance too. From the moment I was born, my parents were adults, and they would stay adults until the day they died. Hence, I couldn't really tell if anything about them had changed over the past ten years. The best I could pinpoint was that the streak of gray hair in my mother's bangs had gotten bigger...but of course, if I said anything about it, she'd probably pinch my eyelids or something.

After that I watched TV for a while, but once I realized I wasn't actually paying attention to anything, I switched it off. Then I opened the sliding glass door to the tiny backyard and caught a whiff of the feeble night wind...so I sat down and let it cool me off.

My body had completely jumped the gun and was already burning with excitement. My parents' house should have been the most relaxing place on earth, and yet, with each passing second the restlessness inside me grew. Was this how everyone else felt the night before a big trip? After a moment, I heard footsteps and looked over my shoulder. The little alien was a shark no longer.

"Classy."

She was wearing that one blue yukata. But her hair was still dripping wet, and she was leaving little puddles of bathwater all over the floor...puddles that seemed to glow as blue as her hair.

"Mama-san has asked me to wear it at bedtime."

Seemingly, every piece of clothing she owned was a gift or hand-me-down. Then again, she couldn't exactly buy any clothes of her own.

"*Mama-san*?" I repeated.

"I am also on such good terms with Papa-san that he will sometimes invite me to go fishing with him," she continued.

"...Are you referring to my parents?"

"Indeed," she nodded. Then she plopped down beside me. "When I inquired as to how I should refer to them, that is what they suggested."

"Interesting."

Personally, I only ever called them Mom and Dad, like my sister did. "Mama" and "Papa" made me cringe a little.

"Everyone in the Shimamura family is so very kind-hearted."

"Apparently so." Only a family like ours would take a random kid in off the street and spoil her rotten. "Hmmm..."

Honestly, shouldn't at least one of us have gotten a little...you know...*concerned* by now? It was one thing to let an unrelated child into the house, but shouldn't we have had second thoughts when we realized she never wanted to leave? And never seemed to age? In that sense, my family was really quite tolerant. Or maybe just apathetic. Not that *I* had any right to judge, I guess.

"Not only that, but Mama-san sometimes gives me cabbage to eat."

"I can't tell if that's a good thing or a bad thing..." *She's not a rabbit, Mom.*

Together, Yashiro and I enjoyed the breeze for a while. Even in the silence, she exuded heat through her flushed cheeks and nose. At this time of night, there wasn't much light shining down on us, and yet, her natural glow lit her up as brightly as the midday sun.

Slowly, it began to dawn on me just what sort of inexplicable being I was seated next to. I would surely never find another person like her anywhere in the world.

"I'm leaving the country tomorrow to go on a trip."

"Ooooh," she replied absently. Then, a beat later, she caved to her own selfish desire: "I shall eagerly await a tasty souvenir."

"I had a feeling you'd say that."

When I looked at Yashiro with her eyes sparkling, I could easily see why my sister kept buying snacks for her. The average person couldn't hope to express joy this pure... unless, of course, they were just as pure themselves.

"...It's so strange, you know?"

"Is it?"

"Yeah." As I combed my fingers through her hair, I contemplated my own emotional state.

Back when I was a not-quite-adult in high school, there was no way Adachi and I could have flown out of Japan. Back then, we couldn't go anywhere—but now, things were different. Now, we could go wherever we wanted. No one would encourage us, but no one would stop us either. If we wanted to go somewhere, then we had to plan for it and put in the effort to make it happen.

At some point, I had jumped from child to adult. This was by no means a one-step process—I couldn't possibly have gotten this far without spreading my wings and taking flight of my own free will, so—

"When was the exact moment I left the nest and became my own person?" I wondered aloud. I had never spoken of this to anyone before.

"The day you met Adachi-san, I would wager," the hungry little fairy-tale creature announced matter-of-factly, without a hint of sympathy for my navel-gazing.

Quietly, I was alarmed that she had an answer at all. I wasn't expecting her to take my philosophical anguish quite this seriously.

"Of all the possibilities presented to you, you will always find your way to Adachi-san," she continued knowingly, as if she were merely recounting what she knew to be fact.

In life, as long as no "undo" button existed, there was only ever one possibility. Nevertheless, Yashiro's frank tone encouraged me to respond candidly in turn. "Really?"

"Yes," she answered quietly, without any fuss or fanfare.

At this point, I was in danger of believing her.

"That is always the point at which you start to change." She put a hand on my shoulder—not a shark's fin or a lion's paw, but her own tiny hand. "Heh heh! You've truly met your match."

Her smug smirk made me giggle. "I guess I have," I admitted, knowing full well that if Adachi were listening, she'd be over the moon right about now. Perhaps this moment was going to waste out here at my parents' house. "Come to think of it...didn't we talk about something like this a long, long time ago?"

"I beg your pardon?"

The way she cocked her head, I was starting to think maybe she forgot. "You told me you thought I was born to meet you."

"Indeed, I did," she replied promptly. Apparently, she *did* remember. "This whole world exists because you met me," she continued casually.

"...Uh, what?"

"Well, you see... How do I explain this? The world as we know it isn't actually all that flexible. The living beings that are born each day, the locations of objects, the food we consume—in most cases, these things are the same across all possible worlds. For example, in order for a banana to be a banana, it has to have the components of a banana, yes? Likewise, the world has all the necessary components. Without them, it would lack the framework needed to exist as a world unto itself. So for the most part, all worlds are fundamentally the same. In summary, this world is designed so that you will always find Adachi-san."

Her voice was still youthful and innocent...and yet, she had become a lot more complicated all of a sudden. Honestly, without any visual aids in front of me, I was only really processing about half of it.

"The only difference between this world and the others is that I am here." Her hair swayed energetically, its color deepened by the shadow of night. "And there is only one of me."

That, oddly enough, was a statement I could agree with...in a way I couldn't quite explain. "You're a real bigshot, eh?"

"Keh heh heh!"

Yashiro was utterly unafraid. Not from courage or overconfidence—more akin to the way we felt no fear toward things we understood, like cell phones or TVs. Perhaps she possessed a similar understanding of the way the world worked. But setting aside whether my suspicions were correct—

"Well, more accurately, I should say it's because *we're* here."

"Huh?"

"And the reason we... No, the reason *I* am here...is because *you* are here. While all versions of you may look the same at first glance, no other Shimamura-san would have sufficed. That is why I believe you were born to meet me."

This conversation wasn't especially complex, and yet, it didn't feel grounded in reality. To her, she was just stating the facts, but her intentions could be thwarted, depending on who was on the receiving end. It could be incredibly difficult to express yourself clearly to another person; one-sided sincerity was simply not enough.

"So basically...it's destiny. Is that it?"

"It is destiny indeed."

Using her pet phrase, we simplified the matter even further.

"Honestly, I don't really understand that sort of stuff."

"Nonsense! It is all quite straightforward!" She set her hand back on my shoulder like a wise old sage. "Heh heh! Truly a special encounter."

...Was it? For a moment, I averted my eyes. What had I gained from bringing Yashiro into my life? Alternatively, if she was right...and I was born to meet her...then what had I really accomplished?

I knew I couldn't truly answer this hypothetical question, and yet, I couldn't help but hop aboard this train of thought just to see where it would take me. All I could see was a tiny glimmer of light on the horizon, and all I had to offer was an ordinary, run-of-the-mill response: I had accomplished having a good time with a friend.

I looked back at her and chuckled. "Yeah, I suppose so." Then I reached out to that tiny glimmer...and stroked her hair.

"Oh, Yachi, there you are!" Just then, my younger sister appeared, wearing her ratty old pajamas with the sloppy sleeves. A hint of steam rose from the gap between her neck and the bath towel slung around it. "Oh, and Nee-chan, too."

"Yep, I'm here too!" I threw up a playful peace sign, but she ignored me.

"Good grief, Yachi, you have to wait until I dry your hair for you! Now the hallway floor's all wet!"

"I was feeling overheated, so I came to cool off. Would you care to join us, Little?"

"And be mosquito food? Pass. Now, look here! I've got *azuki* ice cream for you!"

"Eeeeee!"

When my sister revealed the treat hidden behind her back, Yashiro jumped to her feet and ran to her. This gave me yet another strange sense of *déjà vu*, and as I pondered it, I realized: Adachi had baited Yashiro with ice cream too, just the other day. Then, she scrutinized the small girl and muttered, "What a bizarre little gremlin."

Over the past ten years, Adachi had expanded her circle of friends ever so slightly. Had she taken even greater strides while I wasn't looking?

Alone, I faced off against the night sky. This time tomorrow, I'd be looking up at a different sky in a different country... The thought made my breaths hitch with excitement and a tiny hint of fear. Perhaps it would get easier if I went on more trips—but for now, I decided to let my fears and hopes play out while I yearned for the other side of the sky.

Emotions were best enjoyed in the moment, after all.

The next morning, I quietly ate the shredded cabbage I was offered.

"I'm not a rabbit either, you know..."

Meanwhile, a single shred dangled from Yashiro's lip, dancing in midair.

My sister was still asleep, but I didn't feel the need to wake her just to say goodbye. Chances were high that we'd see each other again at some point during the summer.

The mood was light in the kitchen that morning. The sunlight that streamed in through the window didn't yet possess the power to weigh me down; the faint rays lifted the lethargy from my neck and shoulders and set me free.

After I ate my rabbit food, washed my face, got dressed, and threw on some makeup, I sent a message to Adachi. *"You awake?"*

The reply was immediate: *"What about you? You didn't oversleep again, did you?"*

"If I did, I wouldn't be typing right now," I muttered under my breath. Or maybe she thought I had some kind of superhuman powers. "Hmmm..."

On second thought, I *did* spend every other day practically sleepwalking through my morning routine. A lot of the time, I'd find myself on the train without knowing how I got there. Imagine, if you will, snapping awake to find yourself on a swaying train and nearly losing your balance. This was probably not the sort of experience the average person could relate to.

"I'm gonna head to the airport," I told her.

"Me, too."

I looked at this reply and contemplated the significance of her comma. See, if it were me, I would have written it "Me too." In a way, it reflected our different personalities... These days, I really enjoyed thinking about these sorts of things. Especially in the dark, since it always put me to sleep.

I headed for the front door, and after I gave each of my bags a sturdy pat, I looked over at Yashiro standing beside my mother.

"What is it?" she asked.

Good, there she is.

"Oh, just checking."

Wouldn't want a repeat of last time, after all. I slung my backpack over my shoulder, grabbed the handle of my suitcase, and straightened up. The added weight made me a little unsteady on my feet.

"Well, I gotta get going."

"Yeah, yeah, I hear you."

My mother waved at me dismissively with one hand while she brushed her teeth with the other. Likewise, Yashiro waved a paw—a lion's paw, to be exact.

"Travel safely, got it?"

"Got it."

"And another thing—you really suck at packing, you know that?" my mother sighed as she surveyed the state of my luggage. "I can tell you right now, you won't need all that!"

"Lay off, would you?"

"It will be a struggle to fit all the souvenirs in there," Yashiro chimed in.

I never said I was buying any... Eh, whatever. I'll just buy some chocolates or something. "Hrrrg!" I grunted as I started to drag my heavy suitcase behind me.

"Ha ha, you sound like an old man!"

"Shut *up*!"

My mother was acting like a child, but it was far too much hassle to turn back and deal with her. I opened the door and a silky breeze rolled in, whisking away the last dregs of my drowsiness.

"Hougetsu!"

Annoyed, I turned back at the sound of my first name. My mother was standing there with her toothbrush in her mouth and her arms folded.

"I sure gave you a good name, if I do say so myself!" she announced proudly.

And? So what? I waited for her to continue. But the

only sound was that of Yashiro's flopping tail. "Uh, hello? Your point?"

"That was all I had to say. Run along now." She shooed me away.

"Uh...okay..." And so I left the house. "God, why is she like this...?"

She's always off in her own little world with her own priorities... Then again, they say that about me and Adachi too... No, there's no way we're that *bad...*

"On second thought, that wasn't all."

"Whoa!"

The sudden voice made me jump, and my heavy luggage miraculously jumped with me. My mother was now standing directly behind me, wearing her flip-flops and still brushing her teeth. Yashiro toddled after her, almost as an afterthought.

"Enjoy your trip, alright?"

My mother reached out and aggressively ruffled my hair, swiftly undermining the effort I put in to make it look nice. I started to resist, but then I saw just how thin her arms were and came to a stop.

"All that really matters is that you have fun."

"Okay."

For a while, I stood there and let her mess with my

hair. Once she was satisfied, she grasped the handle of her toothbrush and grinned. "See you." And with that, she went back into the house, her flip-flops clacking with every step.

"Heh. *See youuu*," the little lion echoed, waving. Then she turned and followed after my mother. "By the way, Mama-san, what will you be making for lunch today?"

"Leftovers from last night's dinner."

"Yay!"

"You get excited no matter what I say, don't you? Sure makes my job easier!"

Together, the two of them shared a hearty chuckle. And as I watched the mismatched pair, I realized their smiles were contagious. Now I was smiling too.

"Strange..."

For as long as I could remember, my mother was always an adult, and Yashiro was always a child. Neither of them ever seemed to change; their positions were fixed and immutable. And as I gazed at the walls of the house from a distance, I thought of my sister and father too. That alone was enough to fill my chest with what felt like warm, gentle bathwater.

In the end, it seemed I would never quite "leave the nest" the same way Adachi had.

As mentioned earlier, I hadn't been to the airport since high school. Why did the sight of the timetable and all its text make me giddy? Red partitions extended all the way to the counters, reflected in the polished floor beneath. A tangled mass of footsteps and mechanical sounds and loudspeaker announcements filled my ears. Unsurprisingly for Golden Week, the place was packed.

I pulled out my cell phone and started to message Adachi, since I had a feeling she was already here—

"Shimamura!"

Before I could type a single word, she beat me to the punch—*in person*. I looked up, mildly amazed that I managed to hear her in the middle of this crowd, and spotted her walking my way with a gleeful smile creeping up on her face. Any time the two of us made plans to meet somewhere, Adachi was almost always the first to get there. At times, I felt guilty, but no matter how early I arrived, she was always just a little bit earlier.

She jogged over to me easily, unburdened by her comparatively light luggage. I waved and shouted, *"Hay, gurl!"* in the best American English I could manage.

"Oh, um... *Hi, there*," Adachi replied in English to match mine, though her diction wasn't perfect.

"How would they pronounce your name, anyway? *Adotchy*?"

"Slow down. We're not even on the plane yet."

"*Fine, fine.*"

She had a point; we were still on the ground in Japan. But something in the air smelled distinctly foreign to me, and if even *I* could feel it, despite my total lack of experience outside my home country, then surely, it had to be the real deal. Maybe if I asked Hino, she could explain it to me.

"I brushed up on my English in preparation for the trip, so I figured I may as well practice, that's all."

"I think you'll have to study a little harder than that," Adachi muttered under her breath, but I pretended not to hear it.

Together, we set off side by side, the rolling of my suitcase a pleasing indicator that we were moving forward.

"Your luggage is so huge, it's practically a landmark," she commented.

My mother already made fun of me for this, and I could feel myself starting to pout...but instead, I leaned into it. "I've brought everything we'll possibly need, so feel free to ask me anytime," I declared.

She laughed, then checked her wristwatch. "Looks like we're good on time. In fact, we're actually pretty early."

"Hmmm... Wanna head in and kill time together?"

"Sounds good!" she agreed eagerly. "It's been years since the last time I flew."

I started to nod but froze. "I thought you said you forgot about our last trip!"

"I did, but now I remember." Apparently, her memories flashed on and off like a traffic light.

"Honestly, there's no way either of us could truly forget." After all, it was our first big trip together. "So much happened."

"For sure," she nodded. This time, she didn't try to play dumb.

To be clear, I don't mean to suggest that anything particularly dramatic happened; from an outside perspective, it probably wouldn't seem like much of a special trip at all. It was a perfectly ordinary school trip that Adachi and I got to experience together. Maybe none of it really mattered in the long run. But if the two of us continued to hold the memory of it in our hearts, then surely it had to mean *something*, right?

"Oh, yeah, I'm excited to ride the ferry while we're there!"

"Yeah…"

"And maybe we could do something at the beach."

As I was counting off all the potential plans I hadn't quite made, Adachi smiled faintly. Quietly, I was delighted to see that she had gotten better at expressing herself.

After that, we went through customs, and once we arrived at our departure gate, we spent the rest of our time sitting and gazing through the floor-to-ceiling windows. Children pressed their hands and noses up against the glass, eagerly peering outside; I followed their gazes to the airplane idling in the hangar, then let my eyes wander down the long, perfectly straight runway, squinting in the bright sunshine.

"We've come a long way, haven't we?" I murmured aloud. The sound of it rolled on my tongue, wetting my teeth like a fresh apple.

"We're not even on the plane yet," Adachi snickered in response.

"Yeah, that's true."

Once we boarded that plane, the two of us would go even farther. For now, what awaited me on the other side of the sea was merely a dream…and I was a little over-eager to make it come true.

Together, we would leap into the sky and travel farther than we ever could as teenagers.

2. Our First Trip
PART 1

WHEN I GOT HOME, I found Yashiro toddling down the hallway. Yesterday, she was munching on black edamame beans, but today, she was carrying an entire bunch of bananas. Constantly eating something, this kid. The bright yellow peels paired nicely with her sparkly blue hair.

"Eeeeek!"

For some reason, as soon as our eyes met, she turned and fled back down the hall. Confused, I kicked my shoes off at the door and followed after her. Apparently, she wasn't trying too hard to escape me, because I quickly caught up to her. Then I grabbed her by the scruff of the neck.

"Gyaaah!"

"Why are you running from me?"

"No real reason."

"That's what I thought." I knew she wasn't really the type to avoid someone.

Flailing her legs, she started to unpeel one of her bananas. Her diligent little fingers reminded me of my sister when she was a bit younger. She was a bit more direct with her emotions back then... Honestly, both of us were. But now she seemed to be following in my footsteps.

"Is that your snack?" I asked.

"It is my lunch for the day." She paused to take a bite, then exclaimed, "Tastes like destiny!"

At this time of day, it was a little late for lunch, but Yashiro didn't seem to mind in the slightest. With every bite, her puffed cheeks wiggled happily and her lips quivered with satisfaction. At this rate, I half-expected her to eat the peel too, if I didn't stop her.

"Bananas are very tasty."

"Yes, I know."

"In that case, you may have one."

She pulled one from the bunch and handed it to me. I took it and flipped it over to find the price tag sticker still on it—the same price tags they used at the neighborhood grocery store. I couldn't tell if these bananas were originally ours or not. Then I realized I'd seen Yashiro heading away from the kitchen when I first arrived…

Eh, whatever. I started peeling my banana.

"Is Little still not home yet?"

"Oh, I'm sure she'll be home any minute now." I'd seen clusters of grade-schoolers walking together when I was on my way here, so I figured my sister was probably in one of those groups.

I carried Yashiro to the living room, and when I sat down, she sat down with me. Side by side, the two of us ate our bananas. I hadn't eaten anything since lunch, and the rich sweetness made my cheeks and throat tingle. Meanwhile, Yashiro finished her first banana and started peeling a second. Her body language was exactly that of a small child's. And when I stopped to actually think about it, it was *really* weird that some strange kid was sitting in my house, eating our bananas.

Experimentally, I touched the soles of her outstretched feet. They were as soft as a baby's. When I prodded her sides and her cheeks, I realized they were all just as soft. Almost like she was unaffected by time or the world in general. Not only that, but her skin was faintly chilly like morning dew.

"Mmmh?"

"What sorts of things do you think about on a daily basis?" I was curious about the inner workings of her head. And the outer workings too, of course.

"Usually, I look forward to eating lots of tasty food."

"Ha ha ha ha! Lucky you." Sparkles rose up in a dusty cloud as I ruffled her hair.

"That, and sometimes I wonder how my compatriots are faring."

"Compatriots? Oh, right, I think you mentioned something about that."

I seemed to remember her talking about it around the time we first met, but I couldn't recall any of the details. If I had to guess, she probably meant her family. Previously, she claimed she had come here to look for them, but if so, she didn't appear to be looking very hard.

"I hope they aren't going hungry," she commented matter-of-factly as she started in on her second banana. Frankly, she didn't look that concerned. Apparently, she and her family didn't live together...? In that case, where *did* she live (other than at my house)? Despite her lack of common sense, she spoke perfect Japanese...but her hair color was utterly unnatural...

Whenever I consciously contemplated the parts of Yashiro I normally turned a blind eye to, it drove home just how peculiar she was. It was possible she possessed something that didn't yet exist in humanity's history books...and yet here I was, interacting with her, eating a banana with her. The thought made me feel kind of cool—almost. But it was hard to feel special when I knew she spent every day eating and sleeping.

Then I heard noises at the front door and knew that my sister was home at last.

"She's here."

"Yaaay!" Yashiro flailed her feet in excitement.

Awww, they love each other so much...just like me and Adachi... Wait, but that would make them girlfriends! As her older sister, I think it's a few years too early for any of that... Wait, so I'm fine with my little sister dating an alien as long as they wait a few years?!

I decided not to think about it.

"Oh, hi, Nee-chan. Hi, Yachi."

My sister peeked into the room, her *randoseru* backpack slung over her shoulders. Yashiro sprang to her feet, bananas clutched in one hand, and made a beeline straight to her. Then the two of them did a chest bump. Evidently, this was their idea of a greeting.

"Here's a banana for you too, Little."

"Yay!" Delighted, my sister started eating right away.

"And so another little monkey joins in..."

I'd read somewhere that wild monkeys didn't actually eat bananas at all, but whatever. As I watched over the little peas in their pod, I slumped over my desk and let out a heavy sigh. I wasn't especially tired or anything, but nevertheless, a dull gray curtain of weariness draped over me. Was I just having a bad day? I felt totally drained, as if surrounded by boxes I needed to unpack...

"......"

On second thought, perhaps that metaphor was more fitting than I realized. High school, second year, October, Monday, after school, Adachi. When you added it all up, I had a lot on my plate.

October: the month of school field trips for high school second-years. A lot of schools had planned their big trips around this time, not just ours, or so I heard. Our destination was the same as last year's trip: Kitakyushu, the northernmost city on Japan's Kyushu Island. For an additional fee, students had the option to take a second trip abroad to one of our sister schools in places like Thailand or Australia or the United States—but honestly,

I wasn't interested. One look at my English test scores and I knew *Adachi and Shimamura USA* wasn't going to happen anytime soon.

With the end of the school day fast approaching, the classroom was boiling with energy and body heat. I didn't exactly enjoy it, but I knew I'd miss it once it was gone... and winter was right around the corner... Honestly, the thought was depressing.

Over time, I had come to realize just how much I didn't like winter. It made my body stiff and sleepy, and the time that got wasted to lethargy always seemed to leave a lot of things out to dry. In winter, I needed someone around to hold my hand so I wouldn't freeze to death.

Then I thought about Gon, my grandparents' dog. For now, we were still part of the same world. That alone taught me the true meaning of loneliness; with that knowledge, I would never fully shut the world out. Instead, I closed my eyes and endured the wave of emotions that crashed over me.

As I contemplated all this, the conversation at the front of the room progressed to assigning groups. We were all free to form our own as long as it had five members total, which meant... Sure enough, when I opened my eyes, Adachi had already shot out of her seat, headed briskly in my direction. I had seen this coming, but because she was the first to move, everybody stared at her for a minute.

"What brings you here so swiftly, Adachi?"

I knew the answer to this but wanted to tease her a little. Likewise, she seemed to sense this, as she reached out and grabbed me by the arm. Her nose was flushed pink, and her nostrils flared slightly. Then her mouth began to move.

"Let's...make a group..."

"Okay."

Obviously, this was a foregone conclusion. The only problem was that we'd need to recruit more people to make our group official. Depending on how many students were in our class, the teacher might allow for a four- or six-person group, but definitely not just the two of us. *If only Hino and Nagafuji were in our class,* I thought wistfully to myself, gazing around the room as though this unreasonable wish might spontaneously be granted. The two of them were on somewhat friendly terms with Adachi, so there was a chance they'd all get along...not that they got along amazingly last time...

As my gaze darted around in search of a solution, I could feel Adachi staring passionately at me. Maybe she

was just relieved to be in the same group as me. Knowing her, she had probably spent the entire morning sick with worry. Now, her gaze had softened, with no trace of tension to be seen. *Should I tell her that her mouth's hanging open?*

"Why don't you two join us?"

Just then, the Three Stooges called out to us—uh, I mean, Sancho, DeLos, and Panchos. Not their real names, of course. For some reason, maybe (read: probably) purely to be polite, they had invited us to fill out their roster. I used to talk with them on a daily basis back at the start of our second year, but it fizzled out. Mainly because of Adachi.

"Would that be okay with you?"

"Of course!"

Sancho, the one with glasses, beckoned to us amiably. Unlike Nagafuji, she actually seemed smart and capable... I mean, sure, Nagafuji *looked* smart on the outside, but her brain was basically made of sponge cake.

There were three of them and two of us—exactly five total. Personally, I saw no reason to decline...but of course, there was someone I was forgetting to ask.

"You're okay with it, right, Adachi?"

"Huh?"

She was still gripping my arm, staring into space. When she snapped back to reality, she glanced around at the Trio, then at me. Her gaze was fretful, and her lips were faintly pouty. Apparently, she really wanted it to be just the two of us. This came as no surprise to me, of course, but unfortunately, it just wasn't feasible.

I rose to my feet, stroked her hair, and asked for her clear blessing. "Are you okay with it?"

"...Yeah..."

A few head pats in and she turned into a good girl. Technically, it felt like I'd bribed her into it, but oh, well. Blushing, Adachi retracted her pouted lips ever so slightly. If I kept petting her, I could probably cancel it out completely, but we were kinda in the middle of the classroom.

As the Trio watched us in silence, I turned to them with the best smile I could manage. "This pair of misfits would be happy to join you, if you'll have us."

"Uh...okay," Panchos replied stiffly. Frankly, it was a miracle they didn't rescind their offer.

"Ha ha..."

Right now I didn't feel much like Adachi's girlfriend. I had gone from an older sister to a mother figure.

And so, with our groups now assigned, we were free to go home. The homeroom teacher was still talking about how to pack for the trip, but real talk: there wasn't anything I needed to worry about packing. Heck, I wouldn't even need my street clothes. No need to plan it all out when I could probably just wing it.

Together, Adachi and I left the classroom, but we weren't headed home right away. Instead, we stood in the shade of the bike parking area to talk. I could tell from the look in her eyes that she wanted—no, *demanded*—to have a discussion.

Outside the school building, the sunshine was peaceful and the temperature was mild. I could feel summer's decline against my skin. Tomorrow, we'd take one step closer to the desolation of winter.

"Shimamura, have you ever been to a different country?"

"What? No way," I replied, toying with her bicycle bell. *Do I look like Hino to you?* "I'm not totally opposed to it, though."

Right this moment, all over the world, there were dozens of places I'd never been. At night, while I was drowsily zoning out, all kinds of other things were happening—people laughing, celebrating, mourning, dying, or taking their first breath. There were countless stories I would never know. And when I thought of it that way, the mystery of it pulled me in like a magnet.

Now that we were away from the classroom, Adachi seemed to have recovered. At the very least, she wasn't staring at the ground anymore.

"Where would you want to visit?"

"Oh, I don't know... San Francisco, maybe?"

It was the first place that came to mind—I wanted to see the famous crab wheel at the Fisherman's Wharf. Oh, and I'd heard Croatia had a lot of beautiful cities, so I was interested to see them in person sometime... Perhaps it didn't really matter where I went as long as I could plunge headfirst into the wild blue yonder.

"Th-then let's go there!" Adachi blurted out boldly, clutching my hand in hers.

"Go where?"

"San Fran!"

"Whoa. That's a catchy nickname."

Was it that simple? Could we really go to San Francisco the same way we'd go to the mall or something? No, of course not. San Francisco was farther than Tokyo—even farther than Hokkaido.

"When exactly are we going? Right now?"

"Uh...i-if you want to!"

Apparently, Adachi was dead-set on going on a trip with me. I chuckled. "Nah, I don't think so."

We had school tomorrow, and I didn't have a passport...or, you know, money for an international plane ticket. The average high-schooler couldn't just hop on a plane for a spontaneous getaway for an afternoon or a weekend—especially not to San Francisco. Maybe in ten years or something.

"Hmmm..."

Ten years from now, Adachi would probably still want to be with me...but would I still be with Adachi? I had no way of knowing, but I agonized over it regardless. Anything that wasn't explicitly cut and dried felt deep and philosophical to me.

"Shimamura?"

Adachi peered at me curiously, and I realized I must have spaced out again. I started to wave a dismissive hand, but then...she started fidgeting back and forth.

"It...it's not nice to space out in...the middle of our... conversation," she stammered weakly, her momentum bogged down in molasses. As I gazed back at her, her cheeks promptly flushed pink, the color slowly spreading across her entire face. If I touched her, maybe my fingers would turn pink too.

"Ha ha ha! I love it when you do that."

"Wh-when I do what?"

"When you try to force a joke. It's so cute!"

At this, the pink deepened to red—so bright, not even the shade from the overhang could hide it. She was easy to read in every possible way. Straightforward and unwavering.

"I'm...not forcing it, though..."

"What? You're not? Okay, then, keep 'em coming. I look forward to it!" I laughed.

Backed into a corner, she started to whimper. This too was totally precious.

"Adachi, you scored higher than me on the English test, didn't you?" In fact, I was pretty sure she scored higher than me on basically *every* test. Pretty impressive stuff...or maybe *I* was just really unimpressive.

"I think...you're smarter than I am, though." Her eyes darted restlessly as she attempted to flatter me in turn.

"Don't be silly!" Grinning, I clapped her on the shoulder. It made me realize how much taller she was than me. "I'll count on you to interpret for me."

"I...I'll try my best!"

I was joking, but Adachi took me very seriously.

"What, really? Not gonna suggest we study together or something?"

"Oh... That's way better! Let's do that!" she agreed, shaking our joined hands.

"Sure, I could go for that." I was open to the prospect of expanding my knowledge. That was the kind of optimistic attitude I wanted to maintain going forward.

After a constructive (?) conversation with Adachi...

"Well, then, wanna head home?"

"Okay."

"...Okay, then!" I raised our joined hands. It felt like an anchor, pinning me in place. "Let me go, please!"

"Nnn," she grunted faintly. I could practically hear the joints in her arm creaking stubbornly. "Nnnng...!" Her brow furrowed tightly as her arm shook. *What is she DOING?* Then she used her free hand to pry her fingers away from mine, one by one. She didn't seem to be playing around, either. *Oh, good grief.*

"Are you seriously stuck?"

"I think so," she conceded quietly. But she didn't sound guilty about it in the least—rather, the smile on her face suggested she was quite pleased. She was *enjoying* this. She didn't even seem to care that we were in public. As for me, well...I was used to it, I guess.

Eventually, she managed to pry herself off.

"See you." I waved my newly freed hand. She slowly waved back, and then—

"Uh...*goodbye*," she replied. In English.

"Huh?"

This caught me completely off-guard. Meanwhile, she raced off on her bike. I burst out laughing. *"Hey!"* I called after her in English. "Let's see, uh... *Have a nice day*! Did I get that right?"

Honestly, she probably couldn't hear me. But with this, we had officially started practicing English. How very ambitious of us.

So yeah, that was what happened on my way home after school. I was feeling kinda exhausted after all the social interaction that took place during the field trip group assignment. Once the trip finally rolled around, there was no guarantee that Adachi wouldn't simply take my hand and run off with me. Would I have to play referee between her and the Trio the entire time? *What am I, her little messenger boy?*

"Blegh."

I knew I shouldn't complain, but to be clear, I was no social butterfly myself. Even if Adachi couldn't be everybody's best friend, I really wished she could be just a tiny bit more amiable. That said, her complete and utter disinterest was still...you know...cute. Entertaining. Appealing. Like most of her personality traits. Either way, my primary goal was simply to have fun with her.

Wait—why did I say "messenger boy" when I'm a girl...? Never mind. It doesn't matter.

As I lay slumped over the table, my gaze swayed absently. Whenever I had nothing to do, I was always quick to fall asleep. It was my default state. Were there people in the world who actually *wanted* to spend hours and hours awake and running around?

My vision blurred with my thoughts, and before long, I found myself thinking about Adachi again. She seemed really...*committed*, you know, like she really...*loved* me. At this stage, it finally felt real.

Suppose there were a button that, if pressed, would erase everyone in the world except for me and Adachi, but would give us a house with free food, clothes, and everything we needed to survive. If given the option, there was a chance Adachi would push that button. She couldn't make it entirely on her own, but she'd probably be perfectly happy with just one other person. In a sense, maybe that was proof of her mental fortitude.

As for me, I could handle solitude, but I probably wouldn't enjoy spending all my time with the same person.

I would stay alive, but I wouldn't *feel* alive. I needed two, or three, or four—more than one, at the very least. So if there were a button that erased all of humanity, I would never push it.

This was what I contemplated to myself as I blearily watched the two little monkeys eat their bananas.

A shadow stepped out from the darkness and approached—a blue shadow. *Who's that?* I wondered as I stood there, staring blankly. But I felt no fear, for the shadow wasn't hostile. It merely flailed, demanding my attention. Then, before I could try to determine who it was, the shadow vanished. In its place, a pointed sound pushed up my eyelids and eyebrows.

My body felt warm and heavy, like I'd just drank a tubful of bathwater. This was how I always felt whenever I didn't get enough sleep. I could feel my body fluctuating back and forth between dreams and reality, and the back of my throat was mildly warm, like a sip of tea. I wasn't sleepy—just lethargic.

I'd fallen asleep sitting at the living room coffee table; what woke me was the sound of my phone ringing from inside my bookbag. Who could it be? I rolled over, reached out, and attempted to grab my bag. After a few failed attempts, I flailed my hand harder and harder, pulling a muscle in the process, but whatever. I grabbed it, rolled onto my back, and opened my bag.

In this position, I was reminded of the sea otter plushie my parents bought me from Toba Museum—the one holding the little seashell on its tummy. What ever happened to that thing? It wasn't in my room anywhere. Now I was tempted to go looking for it. But first, the phone call. I checked the screen to find that it wasn't Adachi.

"Oh, hey, it's Taru-chan," I commented to myself in a goofy voice. My legs flailed like a dying fly's, as I spent about five seconds looking for an excuse not to answer. *Coward.*

When I answered the phone, Tarumi spoke right away: "What's up?"

This was her default greeting. She didn't really say "Hello" or "How are you?" or "Pleasant tidings." Then again, did *anyone* say that last one? Maybe a rich girl like Hino could get away with it. Ironically, Hino was more likely to say "Yo" or "'Sup."

Anyway.

"Hey, hey!"

"So, uhhhh...how's it going?"

"Oh, I was taking a nap just now, so I'd say things are going great!"

Tarumi laughed. "You sure do love to sleep, don't you, Shima-chan?"

"Yup. Well, I mean, I don't know if I *love* it. It just sorta *happens*, you know?" I replied in a joking tone.

"There's nothing wrong with that," she told me in her most understanding voice.

"Wait...really?" *You sure you guys aren't letting me off easy?*

"If it's what your heart wants, then that's all that matters...or at least, it's really important... You know, that kind of thing." This was an uncharacteristically serious answer from Tarumi of all people. She fumbled the wording a little, but I could tell that she sincerely meant it. Almost like maybe she was talking about something else entirely. "Sorry, I can't seem to think of the right words today."

"No, no, it's totally fine." I could see what she was getting at, and besides, if she put too fine a point on it, it might come across as preachy. Emotions were better off vague and fuzzy, rather than sharp and clear.

"Oh, yeah, so our school is doing a big field trip soon," she continued, changing the subject.

"Really? Ours is, too."

"Yeah?"

"Yup! Where are you guys headed?"

"Tokyo."

"Didney Worl?"

"No, we're not going to Dizzy Whirl."

Weird how neither of us managed to say that copyrighted name correctly!

"What about you, Shima-chan?"

"Kitakyushu."

"Ohhh, like over by Fukuoka?"

"Yeah, yeah. Then after that we'll go to Nagasaki and... Kumamoto, I think?" I explained, trying to recall the itinerary from memory. For one night, we'd be staying at a hot spring inn too. *I bet it'll smell like sulfur.*

"Are you flying there, or...?"

"Yeah, I think so."

"Guess I'll pray you don't crash!"

"Gee, thanks."

She fell silent for a moment. "Hey, um..."

"Yeah?"

"Once we both get back from our trips...um...wanna hang out again?"

So this was the real reason she called. Likewise, I was

keenly aware of how long it had been since the last time we saw each other. So I started to say yes...but I could feel a *certain someone* holding me back, telling me not to cheat on her. I was anchored to the ocean floor, unable to come up for air.

Yeah...I guess I probably shouldn't.

But I couldn't quite bring myself to explain everything and sever the friendship, either. So instead...

"Maybe sometime."

I didn't agree to it or tell her I would think about it. It was an evasive, cowardly answer. And so, with the question left hanging in the air, I ended the call. Then I stared down at the screen and realized I'd only dozed off for a few minutes at most.

I set my phone down and glanced around. Yashiro was lying on a yellow cushion on the floor, watching a news feature about big-city bakeries. Every time the products were shown on screen, she squealed and kicked her legs in excitement. I looked down and saw that her bananas had been reduced to discarded peels, lying in a pile on the table.

Meanwhile, my sister was peering into her little fish tank and watching her fish. She really loved to take care of them. Plus, she always acted like a big sister around

Yashiro too. As I zoned out, I slumped forward and pressed my forehead back to the table.

"Uggghhh..."

If I asked Adachi, would she give me permission to hang out with Tarumi? No, she'd probably just get mad at me. Not that I had any intention of "cheating" at all, but still, I'd feel guilty going behind her back. To Adachi, it was an unforgivable crime to have any other relationships, even if they were platonic. She was just that obsessed with me. And I was okay with that, but at the same time...

"Love is hard..."

If our love was an anchor, then Adachi was the sea, and I was drowning.

In relationships, did most people look for a partner who possessed the same qualities they did? Or did they look for someone who possessed all the things they were missing? Which was less toxic? Which was "healthy" or "normal"?

Would Tarumi and I fall out of contact again? Just when we had overcome the massive hurdle between us, now another one had taken its place, like the ebb and flow of the tide. Why was life always so complicated? I had fought my way through so many of these problems before now, but clearly, those lessons hadn't taught me anything! I rolled my eyes at myself.

To this very day, I still didn't know what I was supposed to do. I could kinda see the answer in the distance, but I had no clue how to get there from here. And if I couldn't even see ten seconds into the future, then San Francisco in ten years from now was completely out of the picture.

"Only one thing I can do..."

If I didn't feel comfortable talking about Adachi, then I needed to work on that.

That night, I combed through every inch of my room, looking for that sea otter plushie. My sister got annoyed with me, but I ignored her and emptied the contents of every drawer in my search. Unfortunately, I came up empty-handed.

I didn't have many special memories of the school trips I had been on in the past. They just weren't that special. Anything at that level was just a blip in my memory bank; all that mattered to me now was the thrill of the present day and the weight of my body.

All day long, flowers bloomed in my mind—all of them warm colors like red and yellow. I could practically smell their sweet perfume... Every passing minute was spent enduring a deep restlessness in my chest. For me, spring had come early.

Before now, I had never known the beauty of flowers or the intensity of their fragrance, and for a while I wasn't sure what to do...but when I paused for a moment to truly take it all in, my heart grew soft, and I became enraptured by the scent. Over time, I started to realize: *this is what happiness feels like.*

I was going on a trip with Shimamura. Every time I pictured it, I squealed and giggled under my breath. Obviously, something was wrong with me, but I couldn't explain it if I tried. I was so fidgety, I kept looking in the mirror. Naturally, I looked like a freak.

Still, there was one thing that gave me pause: Ideally, I wanted it to be just us. Especially since it was our first-ever trip together! I agonized over it as I headed to work. But right as I passed by the grocery store, I spotted a familiar figure sitting out front, behind a table with a crystal ball—

"Oh."

It was that weird fortune-teller, sitting tall and dignified in the middle of the parking lot...and yet I had a feeling she didn't have permission to be there. Before I could react, however, our eyes met. Then she jumped to her feet and started waving like crazy.

"Hiiii! Hi, there, friend!"

Don't start with me. I averted my eyes and kept going.

"I said *hold it*, you!" She ran up in front of me—how did she manage to be faster than my bike?!

"...Do you need something?" Now that the two of us were face to face, I realized she was actually shorter than me.

"Boy, am I glad to see you! *Konnichiwa*, my *tomodachi*!"

"I'm *not* your *tomodachi*."

But she didn't listen. Instead, she dragged me over to her table and sat me down. Technically, I still had some time before my shift was scheduled to start, but she didn't have to know that. I contemplated using my job as an excuse to slip away... No, she would probably start rambling fortune-telling nonsense at high speed, then force me to pay up at the end. There was simply no getting out of it.

Though she was in a new location, her crystal ball and other decorations hadn't changed one whit. *Must be nice to work wherever you want... Maybe you should invest one of those rolling carts you can pull behind you.*

"Now, then." Once she returned to her seat, the fortune-teller smirked at me through her crystal ball. "How are things going with your little girlfriend?"

It was a rather direct question, and the word *girlfriend* made my legs twitch under the table. Part of it was from embarrassment, but I felt giddy with accomplishment too. The wind had grown stronger with the arrival of autumn, and it tickled my cheek. "Um...good...?"

"I see, I see. So it's been smooth sailing."

"Uh...y-yeah."

"No issues there?"

"Uhhh...nope!" Half-heartedly, I raised my fist.

"No complaints? Not even one?" she pressed, digging further.

"Nngh..." I faltered. "The more you keep asking, the more worried I get."

"Good! Now maybe I can actually do my job!"

Yeah, well, your job sucks. Or maybe it's just you. In contrast with her "friendly" voice and mannerisms, she was quick to change her tune. Hard to believe she meant a single word of it, even the sarcasm.

"Are you *sure* you're not stressed about anything? Really now?" she repeated.

At this point, I could tell I wasn't going to get out of here unless I gave her a problem to solve. *Ugh, if only I'd never met her.* Reluctantly, I decided to get a reading... about the world's biggest non-issue.

"...Well, it's about the big school trip that's coming up."

"Ooh, this sounds juicy." She rolled up her sleeves, eager to get to work.

"Can you tell me what I should pack?"

"Just leave it to me!" The over-eager fortune-teller raised her hands over the mostly useless crystal ball. Then she scowled. "Does it even matter...?" she muttered under her breath.

Ahem. I heard that.

"Enmeyaaah, ho, rah..."

I swear I'm not making this up—she literally started reciting what sounded like some kind of curse. The way it reverberated in the air, it sounded like Tuvan throat singing. First the *takoyaki*, and now this? How many skills did this woman have?

"Yes, it's all coming to me..."

"What is?"

"Be careful not to forget anything. Your lucky color is blue." *What are you, a fortune cookie?* Then she held out her palm as if to suggest the reading was over. "That will be three thousand yen."

"Are you nuts?!"

"Sorry, honey, but I'm the best fortune-teller in town."

"It didn't cost this much last time!"

"Last time, I gave you a first-time discount."

"Okay, well, I don't have my wallet on me."

"Then I guess I'm going to call you Broke Betty from now on!"

"Uh...go ahead...?" If it saved me three thousand yen, it was worth it.

"Anyway, I hope you have fun on your trip."

"Thanks...but still, I wish it was just the two of us... I don't want a million other people coming with us..."

Before I knew it, I had confessed my *actual* problem.

"Oh, please. Can't you just go on another trip with her at a later date?"

"But if it's going to be our first trip together, then shouldn't it just be the two of us?"

Surely, that would be better for both of us. If our first trip together was in a big group, with our *whole school*, we were bound to get distracted with a bunch of other things. It would ruin the sentimental value.

The first experience with something always carried the biggest emotional impact, which then went on to influence related experiences later on down the line. That impact was often immune to the passage of time. Therefore, the first experience was vitally important. And I wanted my first to be with Shimamura. It felt right.

"I see, I see." The fortune-teller nodded pensively, then looked over her shoulder and muttered, "How obnoxious."

I couldn't hear what she said, but I could tell it wasn't polite.

"Well, then, why don't you go on a trip together *before* the big school trip?" she sighed in annoyance as she rolled her sleeves back down.

"Oh…!" It was so simple! But before I could get excited, reality settled back in. "The thing is, I invited her to go on a trip with me the other day, but she said no."

"Hmmm… How did this conversation play out, exactly?"

"I dunno. I was like 'Let's go on a trip today,' or something like that."

"Well, no wonder she said no." The fortune-teller closed her eyes and heaved a big sigh, then donned her customer service smile. "It's important to be considerate of other people's plans. Try inviting her to go on a *Saturday* or something."

"…Oh…"

I was in such a rush, I forgot it was a weekday when I said it. And since Shimamura didn't skip school these days, there was no chance she would have agreed. I had a bad habit of acting without thinking whenever I was flustered… *I should probably work on that…*

"Just relax. Once you've made plans, there's no need to panic. We humans can travel from Tokyo to San Francisco in just ten hours, you know."

My heart skipped a beat. How did she know about San Fran? Did she read my mind?

"Now take action, young one!" She thrust out her fist...then unclenched it and turned it palm-up. "Three thousand yen."

"*No wallet*, remember?"

I rose to my feet. Smiling brightly, she waved goodbye. "See you later, Broke Betty!"

Don't call me that. Without responding, I turned and headed off.

Ultimately, the woman's advice was worth consideration. She was right: the solution was to go on a different trip sooner. That way, I wouldn't *need* to panic about the school trip later.

"Hmmm... *Hmmm...*"

I sat upright on my bed and contemplated when to ask. *Should I just go for it?* My hand hovered over my phone. Would Shimamura think I was annoying? What if she started asking questions? If I tried to explain my reasoning, the conversation would drag on and on, and she'd probably get sick of me... I just couldn't decide.

I knew I needed to take a minute to calm down and get my thoughts in order...but looking back, I had yet to successfully maintain my composure whenever Shimamura was involved. Maybe I traded it in at some point for all these pretty flowers in my head. In the end, I switched my brain off and wrote her an email:

"May I call you?"

The second I sent it, I realized I could have simply typed out my entire proposal and sent it to her that way. But whatever—I wanted to hear her voice. A short while later, my phone started to ring. Instead of writing me back, Shimamura had skipped a step. I answered immediately.

"Sooo what's up?" she asked.

She sounded normal, which came as a huge relief. I had scaled a wall with my bare hands to see if I recognized what lay on the other side. Shimamura was my homeland; every time we were together, I felt as though I truly belonged. The smell of flowers engulfed my nose.

"Well, I was wondering..."

"Yeah?"

"Would you wanna go on a trip with me this Saturday?"

"I want a souvenir. A *luxury* souvenir."

"Only if you behave yourself while I'm gone."

On the morning of the school trip, my kid sister stood in the hallway in her pajamas, watching as I stepped into my shoes. In place of her usual pigtails was a major case of bedhead.

"I know you're gonna miss me, but try not to cry, okay?"

"Not happening! Hyah!" She kicked me in the butt.

"Gyah!" In revenge, I reached out and pressed my palms hard against her temples.

"Hgggnnhh!" She flailed her legs in protest.

After I had my fun with her, I let her go. Maybe now she was a little more awake.

"Wait a minute... Where did Yachi run off to?" she murmured to herself, rubbing her eyes as she looked over her shoulder. "I thought I just saw her in the kitchen."

"Seems like she's *always* in the kitchen, if you ask me." *That's what you people get for feeding her. Wait, but I was the one who started it... Oops.*

I waved goodbye to my sister, then left the house. Outside, I was met with the last lingering traces of summer's warmth. But while the temperature hadn't quite caught up with the times, the sky above had already made the transition to autumn.

October mornings started out fuzzy indigo blue, with thinly shredded clouds overlapped in layers. At first, the houses across the street were cloaked in shadow, but as the sun rose, their windows began to shine. I breathed in the light and felt a flame rise up inside me. This was but a tiny glimpse of the scenery on Planet Earth.

On a day like today, you'd think Adachi would come to pick me up, but this time, I was on my own. I adjusted my grip on my backpack straps. "All right, let's go," I announced to no one in particular. And with that, I headed off to school.

There I would find my hopelessly stubborn girlfriend waiting for me.

When I arrived, the buses were already parked in front of the school building. They would take us to the transit center, where we would catch the airport shuttle. Our town was so rural, it required two separate bus rides to get there.

The buses were emblazoned with the town mascot's cheeky grin. As I approached, I followed the sounds of students chatting until I spotted a group gathered together; Hino and Nagafuji were among them.

"Yo, Ma-chee!" Hino greeted me casually. At this point, you couldn't even tell the nickname was derived from my name.

"Good Shima-morning!" Nagafuji chimed in. Surprisingly, hers made more sense. Then she let out a big yawn and pulled her glasses off.

"This ditz rearranged her suitcase *three times* before we went to bed. Can you believe it? We hardly got any sleep!" Hino complained.

"Ha ha ha..." To be honest, I wasn't in any position to judge.

"Good thing I spent the night at your house. That way, I didn't end up late for school! Heh heh heh!" Nagafuji declared proudly.

"Oh, yeah?" I asked.

"Look here, you," Hino spat, glaring up at her. "Quit coming over to my house without asking! You know I don't like it!"

"Whyzat?" Nagafuji blinked.

"Lots of reasons!" Hino waved her hands emphatically

while Nagafuji peered at her in confusion. Honestly, after how my mother reacted when Adachi came over to spend the night with us, I could kind of guess why.

"You've got a lot of stuff there, Shima-Shima. You excited for the trip?"

I see I've gained an extra Shima. "I don't know about *excited*... I just wasn't sure what I'd need, so I kept adding stuff..."

"Oh, and if you're looking for Ada-chee, she's over there," Hino informed me, pointing into the distance. Sure enough, I could see the back of Adachi's head, along with her backpack. Unsurprisingly, she was standing all by herself.

"Cool, thanks."

"See you later, Shima-Shima-Shima!"

One Shima is enough, thank you very much. I waved goodbye and headed off to see Adachi. Behind me, I could hear Nagafuji asking, "Whyzat? Whyzat?" over and over.

As I approached, you'd think Adachi would notice me and jog up with a smile, but...she didn't. Things between us were a little strained at the moment. For some inexplicable reason, she had decided that she wanted us to go on a trip of our own ahead of the school trip. Naturally,

I declined—but then she got mad and started sulking. Honestly, it was impossible to parse just what was going through her head.

"Good morning," I greeted her, as if none of it had ever happened.

She stiffened up slightly. "Hey."

Apparently, she was still in a bad mood. *Oh, you.* Smiling, I shook my head. She reminded me of my little sister whenever she threw a tantrum, and I wasn't too worried. She'd get over it eventually.

After a while, the teachers directed us to board the buses. The only requirement was to sit with our assigned group, so naturally, Adachi and I ended up next to each other. We were seated near the back, directly over the rear axle.

After the bus started moving, I peered across the aisle at the seat beside us—*eh, they probably won't notice.* Facing forward, I surreptitiously took Adachi's hand in mine. (In the process, I accidentally touched her thigh, but I wasn't trying to grope her, I swear.) I felt her soft hand flinch against my palm and smiled at her.

"Let's try to have fun, okay? It's a special occasion."

Now that we were in high school, this would be our last chance to go on a school-sanctioned trip. Compared to the rest of our boring adult lives yet to come, the memories we were about to make had the potential to be unforgettable.

Adachi sucked in a breath. Then, finally, she squeezed back.

"We can't wipe the slate clean, but for now, let's sweep it all under the rug. Then after we come home, we can worry and fight and sulk all we want. Deal?"

Honestly, I wasn't the type to switch gears that easily... and after getting to know Adachi, I knew she wasn't, either...

"Alternatively, if you need help having fun on the trip, I could... Let's see... I'll smile at you the whole time!" I declared, picking what I hoped was the most effective tactic. She widened her eyes at me, but nevertheless, I beamed back at her. As you might expect, she blushed and looked around anxiously. Then, at last, she giggled. *Cutie.*

"Look, um...I'm sorry," she mumbled as her shoulders slumped. Evidently, she felt bad about getting grumpy with me.

"Ha ha ha! No worries—it's fine. The trip only just started, so you're right on time," I grinned. She looked back at me bashfully.

And so our high school trip officially began. Our destination: Kitakyushu. It was the autumn of my second year, and for the first time in my life, I would touch the sky.

Truth be told, it was my first time visiting the airport too. I kept glancing around fretfully like a lost tourist, and when it came time to actually board the plane, my composure sprouted wings and flew away. As I sat there, the noise steadily grew louder and louder until eventually I started to worry that the whole thing might in fact explode. I could hear the sharp *whhhf whhhf* of something slicing through the air, over and over.

Then the plane started to move. My head rattled from the motion, and the scenery outside started to sway. We had turned onto the runway.

"Ohh!" I exclaimed under my breath as we began to pick up speed. The momentum was pushing me back against the seat. Then the deafening sounds converged, and my body—along with the body of the plane—began to tilt upward.

Liftoff.

Reflexively, I gritted my teeth. I half-expected my seat

to go hurtling through the air. The view from the window was now diagonal as the plane seemed to roll up an invisible incline. My legs swung through empty air beneath my seat. And so, unhindered by gravity's pull, we began to fly.

Around the time my palms were slick with sweat, the captain told us over the intercom that we had reached cruising altitude. Confused, I glanced around. It was still so loud and cramped... Really, there wasn't much about this situation that I enjoyed at all.

As the antsy feeling in my chest persisted, Adachi reached out and took my hand—just as I had done for her on the bus, except decidedly less sneaky about it. Maybe it's weird, but I was impressed by her confidence... and likewise embarrassed that my fear was now blatantly obvious. I debated whether to say something, but she stared straight ahead with a peaceful look on her face. She seemed to enjoy holding hands with me regardless. So I closed my mouth, adjusted my sitting position, and faced forward.

My pulse was racing faster than the propellers on the plane's engines. Together, we were holding hands...while 40,000 feet in the air. Strangely enough, the thought put a smile on my face.

As we descended, I gazed out at the city of Kitakyushu and its surrounding mountains and prayed desperately that we wouldn't crash. Naturally, we didn't. After we landed, my heart continued to thump in my chest, and the familiar feeling of gravity sent a shudder down my spine. As it turned out, flying was no easy feat on this planet. Suddenly, I had a newfound respect for birds.

Once we had deboarded, we walked along in a big group. A short while later, my ears popped, and all the previously muffled sounds came rushing in at once. Loudest of all were the shouts and laughter of my classmates. Now I was starting to feel dizzy.

"Flying's a lot more peaceful in my dreams..."

"Huh?"

"Nothing."

Adachi would inevitably hear even the faintest of whispers, so I had to stay on guard... *Wait, what am I saying? I can't even relax around my own girlfriend?*

In my own defense, though, anyone would want to impress someone they liked in the hopes of being liked in return. It was perfectly natural to be a little nervous.

Sounds exhausting, to be honest. Why is love so complicated?

We walked through the airport for what felt like an eternity before we finally reached the ground floor lobby. From there, we split into our assigned groups and waited for the teachers to give us our next instructions. Those who needed to use the restroom left their suitcases with their friends and rushed off.

I guess a lot of different schools are here at the same time as us, I mused to myself as some other students walked past in the distance, all wearing dark-green uniforms. Our local agricultural high school had green uniforms too, but in a lighter shade.

My gaze darted to and fro. I was so far removed from my sphere of daily life, and yet...there weren't many new sights or smells. Everyone was speaking Japanese, and the crowd was sweltering, and the weather outside was bright and sunny... Honestly, I was expecting at least one thing to be drastically different from home, so for me, this was a bit of a letdown.

"Do you need to use the bathroom, Adachi?"

"No...?" She pouted her lips at me. "Are you treating me like a little kid?"

"Well, I sure wasn't *trying* to," I answered cheerfully.

But just then, as I adjusted my backpack, I heard a muffled sound: "Ghhnn!"

"……"

A cold sweat trickled down my back.

"Shimamura?"

I jumped up and down three times on the spot.

"Ghhgg!" came the muffled but otherwise unruffled response. Sure enough, it was coming from my backpack. Now my face was sweating, too.

"Sorry, uh… I'll be right back," I told the rest of the group.

But a certain pair of footsteps refused to leave my side. When I turned back, Adachi was following after me, staring at her shoes. I felt like a mother duck.

"I need you to go back and wait with them," I explained.

"Huh? How come?"

"Because I'll only be a minute!"

When I reached out and stroked her hair, she thrust her head at me, demanding more…so I gave her more. Her lower lip quivered as she savored the moment.

"Pet, pet…"

Now my hand was starting to go numb. *Ugh, I'm gonna be stuck here forever!* When I pulled away, her shoulders flinched upward, chasing after my fingers. Then, as I gazed straight into her eyes, I realized just how much taller she was… *Hmmm. Did she gain another inch over the past year?*

"Adachi, I'd really appreciate it if you could do as I ask, just this once," I explained as gently as I could manage.

But she must have thought I was criticizing her, because her loving smile went stiff. "Sorry, um—I'm not trying to be difficult or anything, but...I just don't think we're supposed to split up..." At first, she stumbled over her words in haste, but after a moment, she faltered and started to fidget.

"No, no. Seriously, I'll only be a second, I promise. Be right back."

With a wave, I hurried off; she stood there and watched me go. I started to have second thoughts—did it really matter if Adachi saw? Then again, I couldn't risk making this trip any more complicated than it already was.

"Now, then..."

I concealed myself behind the escalator and lowered my backpack. Then, once I was sure no one was watching, I summoned all my courage and unzipped it. A head of sky-blue hair popped up from inside, like a baby bird peeking out from its nest.

"Good morning!"

"............"

Simultaneously, I was struck with two conflicting thoughts: *This has to be a joke* and *Oh, god, I knew it.*

A sandstorm rose up in my chest. As I stared down at her at a total loss for words, she turned her head from side to side, peering around curiously. "Where are we, exactly?"

I'm the one who should be asking questions right now, thank you very much! "This is the airport. The Kitakyushu airport."

"I see, I see." From the way she nodded, I could tell she had no idea what I was talking about.

"So anyway, first things first... Right, uh, what are you doing in my backpack?" Honestly, there were a lot of other questions that came to mind, but hopefully this one was the most important.

"Well, you see," Yashiro began casually, as though nothing was amiss, "when I visited your house this morning, I found this backpack just sitting there."

"Uh huh?"

"And I just so happened to climb inside."

"What, on accident?"

"And then I just so happened to fall asleep."

"I'm seeing a pattern."

"And now here I am!" she exclaimed gleefully, raising both hands into the air.

How did she make it through customs? For that matter, how did she fit her whole body into my regular-sized backpack? And what happened to the stuff that was supposed to be in there? At this point, she wasn't just weird—she was *terrifying*. My only option was to try not to think about it too hard.

"Well, I can't expect you to go home on your own, and I can't really be seen walking around with you, so...wanna stay in there?"

I felt pretty weird for suggesting it, but weirder still, she actually *agreed*. "Yes, I think I shall."

"No peeking out from inside without my permission, okay?"

"Oh, you needn't worry about that. I shall sleep until I am called upon. Ho ho ho!"

If only I could be as laid-back about this as you are.

"By all means, think of me as your own personal Nezuko."

"Oh, yeah? Should I get you one of those bamboo muzzles too?"

I zipped my bag up and slung it back over my shoulders. She was so light, it really didn't feel like I was carrying another person. In fact, she was scarcely a burden at all...except on my mind, I guess.

"Are you gonna need snacks, or do you have some?" I decided to ask, just in case. Couldn't let her drop dead in there, after all.

"I'm okie-dokie, artichokie."

"Wow. Haven't heard that one in a while."

"But I *would* enjoy eating some fruit if you should happen to acquire some."

"Yeah, yeah, I'll think about it."

If they found out about her, would I go to jail for child abduction? Frankly, I wasn't confident I'd be able to talk my way out of it.

"Sorry for the wait!"

When I made it back to my group, Adachi zipped right up next to me like a magnet. Then our group started walking, but...we weren't exactly a cohesive unit. The two of us were divided from the rest, all thanks to Adachi putting up a wall between us.

I felt bad, since the Trio went out of their way to invite us to their group in the first place, but this was simply who she was. It just wasn't realistic to expect her to play nice. Although from *her* point of view, she *was* playing nice... I could only lament the many complex facets to this issue.

This airport felt basically identical to the one I departed from; the heavy heat dried out my sinuses. If this were another country, would the weather and scenery make me feel like I was in a whole new world? How many times had Hino experienced something like that? We had both spent the same number of years on this earth, and yet her lived experience was completely different from mine. Not to suggest that my experiences weren't just as important, of course. I wouldn't trade them for the world.

As I mulled it all over, we stepped outside, where the bright daylight streamed down at an angle, but I didn't mind. To me, sunshine always seemed to mark the start of something new. Then we boarded another bus and traveled a long, long distance from the airport...but I must have nodded off at a few points, because I could only remember bits and pieces. Easier to sleep on a bus compared to an airplane, after all.

As I shook myself awake, however, I noticed Adachi hunched over, looking down at her phone and blushing. She was staring so intensely, I got curious and took a peek. And when I did, I came face to face with...myself. A photo of myself, asleep. Which Adachi had set as her wallpaper.

In the photo, my eyes and mouth were closed and I was resting my head against the window pane. *I look so peaceful,* I thought to myself with a hint of envy. (Maybe it was weird to be jealous of myself, but I could never relax that much when I was awake.) Also, I was relieved to see that I wasn't drooling. According to my mom, I did that a lot.

"It's not often I get to see what I look like when I'm asleep," I commented aloud.

At this, Adachi nearly leapt out of her skin. Panicked, she whirled around to look at me, already sweating bullets.

"It's not polite to take creepshots, Sakura-chan. Ever heard of publicity rights?" I complained, though I didn't know if *publicity rights* even applied in this situation.

She whipped her head from side to side, strands of hair slapping against her nose and cheeks. Honestly, it looked painful, but at the same time, it was kind of funny, so I let her keep going for a while. Then, at last, she hung her head in defeat. "I'm sorry."

"It's okay. I don't really mind." After all, I must have looked unbearably adorable while I was asleep...right? "So what made you want to snap a pic?"

I was curious to learn what, if anything, inspired her to capture that particular moment. She recoiled, as if to suggest this was an audacious question to ask. It seemed she wasn't comfortable telling me... Now I was *really* curious. *Hopefully, I can get it out of her before we arrive,* I thought to myself as I glanced out at the scenery.

Then she put her fists in her lap and answered in a tiny voice, "I...I thought you looked really pretty." Not only were her lips trembling, her *ears* were trembling, too. No clue how she managed that.

"Pretty? Me?"

She nodded meekly.

"Wow. Nobody's ever really said that about me."

There were several instances in which Tarumi had called me *cute*, though. I paused to think about her. Just when we had finally rekindled something, now it was falling apart all over again. But I didn't want to admit it, which was proof of just how much it was affecting me on the inside.

"That's...probably a good thing," Adachi muttered.

At first, I didn't understand what she was referring to, and since I couldn't read her mind, it took me a minute to piece it together. "I beg your pardon?!" Was Adachi some kind of heartless monster who didn't like it when other people got compliments?

"Well...when you're pretty...people tend to flock to you," she mumbled, peeking up at me with her damp eyes like she was testing the waters.

Oh, so that's *what you meant... Wait, so I'm not pretty after all? Ouch.*

"Er, but you really *are* pretty, though! People just don't tell you to your face because...uh...they're shy!"

"It's okay. You don't have to try to make me feel better."

Frankly, Adachi herself was way prettier than I was, but she wasn't really the type to appreciate those sorts of compliments. Then again, if *I* said it, she'd probably blush beet red... *I guess she really loves me,* I thought to myself bashfully. If I had to guess, it was that same love that inspired her to take a photo of me... *Wait, that gives me an idea.*

"All right, my turn. Can you fall asleep for a sec?"

"Huh?!"

At first, she flinched back in horror, but a few moments later, she obediently closed her eyes. I was mostly joking, but I appreciated her willingness to cooperate. Her brow was furrowed, and I could practically hear her silently commanding herself to fall asleep. Admittedly, I wanted to see if it would actually work, so I watched with my phone at the ready. *If you can pull this off, I'm gonna call you Nobita-kun from now on.*

Alas, after a few strained grunts, she reluctantly opened her eyes and looked back at me in defeat. "Sorry...I can't."

"I kinda figured." Grinning, I clapped her on the shoulder. "Okay, then, let's get a pic of you smiling."

"Huh?!"

For some reason, she was acting like this was somehow *more* unreasonable than the last request. *Gimme a break.* I held up my phone. "Say cheese!"

"Uhhh...okay..."

At my prompting, she donned what I could only assume was her best attempt at a smile—eyes wide, corners of her mouth twitching, frozen like a deer in headlights, her nose twitching in sheer terror. If I took this picture, people would think I was holding a gun to her head just off screen. As I debated whether to give her a gold star for...uh...effort, she began to sweat.

"Your smile looks a little forced." *Probably because I'm literally forcing you.* "I guess you haven't had much practice, have you?" Looking back, I knew she was at least capable of a derpy grin. That one was pretty cute.

But in her second attempt at a normal smile, her lower lip quavered. She squeezed her eyes shut in defeat. Then her chin jutted out, and her lips splayed in opposite directions, until eventually her expression didn't resemble a smile in the slightest. Still, I liked the look of it, so I decided to snap a pic regardless. She heard the shutter sound effect and timidly opened her eyes.

"Uh...d-did I get it?"

"No, not really," I replied, smiling.

Blushing faintly, she cocked her head in confusion. "What?"

"Don't worry about it."

I navigated to the photo I took. Sure enough, there she was in all her awkward glory. Now we could both have pics of each other as our wallpaper... *Eeee, we're totally girlfriends! I love technology!*

"Hey, uh, Shimamura?!"

"Yeah?" Beyond my phone screen sat Red Adachi in the flesh.

"I know I'm not great at smiling, but I really do have lots of fun when I'm with you. And I know sometimes I get all flustered and stuff, but...uh, I'd like it if...if I could learn to express myself better!" she confessed, her lips trembling along with her gaze. But her sentences didn't connect quite so seamlessly—a fitting metaphor for Adachi as a person.

At point-blank range, her sentiment threatened to heat up the entire bus. But of course, Adachi wasn't the type to worry about other people overhearing her.

"Well, uh...I'm glad to hear it," I replied, slightly embarrassed. She hadn't stopped blushing either. But if I chose to ignore all the same things she did, perhaps we could have a fun bus ride after all.

This was quite possibly my first time going out over the ocean. Gripping the ferry railing, I closed my eyes and felt my body swaying with the waves. The wind that brushed past my ears seemed to bite a little harder, and the darkness behind my eyelids swirled around in circles. But I felt no fear.

"Sleepy?" a voice remarked beside me. Scowling, I opened my eyes and looked over.

Adachi looked back at me with wide eyes, holding her hair flat as the wind ruffled through it. On the whole, she could come across as quiet and mature, but when you paid attention to the small details, you started to catch glimpses of her inner child. And when she looked at me with her eyes as round as saucers, she reminded me of my little sister.

"*C'mon*, Adachi. Don't ruin it!"

I spread my arms wide, trying to convey "it" without words. We were on a ferry, purposely taking the scenic route to our destination. All around us, we could hear our classmates having fun. Out here on the deck of this huge ship (okay, probably not that huge), the ocean seemed to stretch on endlessly in a blur of blue and white. I wasn't "sleepy"—I was just trying to take it all in. Sure, I woke up really early today, and the fatigue was seeping into me like sea water, but I still didn't appreciate the accusation. *Blunt honesty isn't always a virtue, you know.*

"Oh, were you, like...having a zen moment?" she asked, blurting out the first thing that seemed to fit without stopping to think about it.

"Yeah, totally. Might start doing yoga poses next."

Weird, how traveling always brought out my sentimental side. I peered out over the railing and watched as the ship's bright white hull sliced through the water. Now and then the spray would fly high, misting our cheeks and bringing a sharp, salty smell to my nose—the smell of the sea, I guess.

"It finally feels like we're on a trip somewhere, doesn't it?"

I guess my mental image of traveling involved a boat ride. Not only that, but it felt like I was *home*. But if so... what did that make my actual home?

The other students were busy feeding the seagulls with packets of cereal they received from the ferry employees. Evidently, these birds were used to tourists, because they flew down and caught each piece in midair without missing a single one. As I watched, I thought to myself: *I bet*

Yashiro could do that. Not that I would feed her old, stale cereal.

The gulls kept flying really close to us. Suddenly, one shot past my face; when I flinched in surprise, it got spooked and flew away.

"So do you like boats?"

"Well, it's my first time riding one." *But I'm enjoying it ferry much! Get it? Because...we're on a ferry... You know what, I'm gonna keep that one to myself.* "But I hope I get another chance someday," I continued, letting my hopes fly on the wind like a drifting balloon.

"Then let's make it happen," Adachi replied, catching it by the string. Her words were firm, with no room for negotiation.

"Sounds good."

I leaned my upper body against the railing and gazed beyond the bowsprit to our destination. In the greater scheme of things, this was just a tiny glimpse of the ocean, and yet, I felt as small as an ant. I could see everything and nothing all at once. And in that moment, I felt like I was adrift at sea—alone.

I shivered in the chilly sea breeze.

From there, we deboarded at the ferry terminal, and a short while later, we were at a park so famous, I already knew its name. Technically, it wasn't a "park" at all—it was a shrine or something, and it was known for having a great view of the ocean and other scenic attributes. But we didn't come for any of that—we were just here to eat lunch.

The first floor was a souvenir shop, and the second floor was the dining area. Each group headed up the stairs and sat together at one of the provided picnic tables; when I sat on the edge of the bench, naturally, Adachi swooped in next to me. On a whim, I reached out and combed my fingers through her bangs. She looked at me in confusion.

"Oh, it's nothing. Just felt like it," I told her.

"I don't believe you."

Secretly, I couldn't help but think of her as a loyal Labrador retriever.

I set my backpack down on the ground next to me—gently, lest Yashiro make any more weird grunting sounds. Our lunch today was *shabu-shabu* with *soba* noodles and horse meat, the latter of which I had never tried before. Now that I thought about it, I was having a lot of first-time experiences on this trip... Using my chopsticks, I plucked up a slice of horse meat and marveled at how thinly it was cut. Did my lack of sympathy for the horse make me a heartless monster?

"Do you like horse meat?" Adachi asked as I scrutinized it at eye level.

"I've never had it."

"Oh. Me either." She beamed brightly. For a second, I was confused why this elicited such joy from her, but then it clicked.

She likes it when we have stuff in common. Wait, so she only likes people who are the same as her...? No, that's not it. She doesn't really seem to like herself, but she does *like me. Therefore, the two of us must not be that similar... But in that case, why does she always want me to see things her way?*

As I contemplated this contradiction, I slurped my noodles and relished the grainy mouthfeel. The flavor of the horse meat, however, was overstaying its welcome. Then, after I chewed for a while, I realized I was meant to dip it in the sauce first.

Likewise, Adachi ate her noodles in silence. Was she physically capable of enjoying food at all? I certainly couldn't picture it. Not long after I started watching her, she sensed my gaze and looked back at me, her eyes shimmering with anticipation. *So cute.*

"It's nothing, really," I told her.

"Now I *super* don't believe you."

The meal came with two sliced apples for dessert. Experimentally, I plucked up a slice with my chopsticks and surreptitiously held it out to my backpack. Before I could even unzip it, a pale appendage (hand?) shot out from inside and snatched the apple slice. *Freaky!* Then, when I listened closely, I heard the sounds of crunching, followed by a tiny "Tastes like destiny." *Nope, still freaky.*

I tested it again with another slice. Once again, she snatched it away in a flash. *No one's watching this, right?* I wondered nervously. But despite my best efforts to stay cool, I could feel my face tensing up.

Nonchalantly, I glanced around. Just then, I made eye contact with Nagafuji sitting at the table across from ours. She slid her glasses back on, which made her look about 30 percent smarter overall, and rose to her feet. Then she picked up her bowl of noodles and headed my way. *Wait, why are you bringing your food?* Glasses or no glasses, she never made much sense to me.

She proceeded to walk *alllll* the way around until she was standing directly behind me; I looked up and came face to face with her boobs. Up close, they were *ginormous.* Like two meteors crashing to Earth. *Okay, maybe it's not that deep.*

"Hmmm…" She peered down at my backpack.

Oh, god, she totally saw us.

"Sheemura-chan, did something crazy just happen, or am I blind?"

At this, my brain offered three different responses:

OMG, what are you talking about, silly?

Uh, you must have been seeing things.

Heh. Everything's crazy whenever you're around.

But most importantly, I needed to take into account exactly who I was speaking to.

"Did it?" I asked.

"Well, I sure hope so!"

Don't hope for that, you weirdo. "Remind me: How bad is your eyesight?"

"I'm 20/200 in both eyes. Yaaay." She threw up a half-hearted peace sign.

"Well, then, can you really trust anything you see without your glasses?"

"You're right. I can't."

She agreed so readily, it threw me for a loop. Classic Nagafuji. With that, she bade me farewell and walked off with her noodles. "The heck were you doing?" I heard Hino ask once she returned to her seat.

"What was that about?" Adachi asked me, like she was my own personal Hino.

"Beats me," I replied, tilting my head. "Nagafuji's always sort of an enigma."

That was my cover story. Frankly, I was lucky Nagafuji was the one who caught us. I snuck a glance at my backpack and was relieved to confirm that Yashiro wasn't peeking her little blue head out. I couldn't hear any more crunching either.

"*Sheemura-chan*," Adachi mumbled into her noodles. Then, stiffly, she turned to me and tried it out for herself. "Sh-Sheemura...?"

"Kinda sounds like *zebra*," I remarked.

"Yeah..."

So neither of us thought it was a fitting nickname. What would a Zebra-mura do, anyway? Did zebras neigh? Idly, I tried to remember if I'd ever seen one IRL.

There was this one time my family went to the zoo, and my favorite part was listening to all the birds singing in the aviary. My sister was only two or three back then, so she probably didn't remember it, but I could recall my mother pointing at each of the animals and teaching her what their names were. No memories of any zebras, unfortunately. The mystery of the stripey horse would have to wait.

"Hey, Adachi? Can I have one of your apples?"

"Uh, sure..."

I only asked for one, but she handed me the whole plate. *Oookay, then.* I took it—and the second she looked away, I snuck it down to my backpack. With a *whoosh*, the slices all disappeared, and for a second it really sank in: *This is nuts.*

"Thanks," I said as I handed the empty plate back to Adachi. She stared down at it in shock and disbelief.

"You already finished?"

"Gobbled 'em right up!" I answered brightly to drown out the faint sounds of crunching in my backpack.

After we finished our lunch at the park, we left without doing any sightseeing. Then we boarded another bus for the Hell Tour—no, seriously, that's what it was called. We walked from place to place without pausing to linger for even a moment. Oh, but at one point, we saw a bunch of alligators. Easily the highlight of the tour.

"Shimamura, are you an animal lover?" Adachi asked, possibly because I kept staring at the gators.

"You know, I think I might be," I nodded, thinking of Gon, and the zoo, and...

"...Shimamura?"

Would it be rude to count Adachi as one of my favorite creatures?

After the Hell Tour, we traveled to the hot spring inn, where we would be staying for our first night. As I approached the stairs out front, sure enough, I could already smell the sulfur. It wasn't an inherently pleasant scent, and it plagued us all the way to our group's assigned room. Did all hot springs stink this bad?

Inside, the walls and *tatami* mats had gone yellow from sun exposure. The light fixture was dim, casting shadows in the corners of the ceiling. In this old-fashioned room, the brand-new TV stuck out like a sore thumb.

As for the Trio, they appeared to be worn out from all the walking, because they were lounging around without bothering to open their suitcases. I set mine down against the opposite wall. What if I needed to open my backpack to get something? What would happen if I reached inside?

Hmmm... Could I ask everybody to leave real quick? Wait, better idea: Maybe I could have Yashiro sneak me my stuff?

As soon as Adachi was out of range, I made my move. "Could you give me some clean clothes?"

In a *whoosh*, the pale hand-appendage emptied the backpack's contents at me—literally *all* of my clothes, plus my travel itinerary. *Does this look like clothing to you? Where do you expect me to wear it?*

"Put this back."

At my request, the little hand snatched up my itinerary and retracted it back inside. In a sense, this system actually made things *easier*, since neither of us had to put in much effort. I decided to reward her with whatever they gave us for dessert tonight.

But while I was having a grand old time with my backpack buddy, Adachi looked at me in puzzlement. "Shimamura? Are you gonna get changed or something?"

"No, no, I'm just...uh...reorganizing." I swiftly folded them into a stack, then looked up at her and played it off with a giggle.

"Wh-what's so funny?"

"Oh, I was just noticing that you've cheered up, that's all."

She was totally sulking at the start of the trip, but now she was back to her normal self. When I pointed this out, however, she started to shift around on her feet, as did the shadow she cast over me. "Well, because...y-you..."

Fidget, fidget, fidget. Evidently she hadn't completely gotten over it. But to be honest, I didn't get why she was so hung up on it in the first place. And even if I asked her to explain it, I probably wouldn't comprehend more than half of it. I couldn't always relate to her priorities. But hey, maybe that was what made our relationship fun.

"I can't promise it'll happen anytime soon, but...we should go on another trip sometime, just the two of us."

"When?" she demanded, like a little kid who was skeptical of a grown-up. But I didn't have a concrete answer for that.

"Um...after we graduate?" I suggested vaguely. She shot me a look that said, *That's forever from now*, so I continued, "Look, if I'm being honest, I don't have the money for a big trip, okay? That's why it has to wait until after I graduate and get a job."

Without missing a beat, she pressed a hand to her chest. "I'll pay for it!"

Fun fact about Adachi: despite her antisocial personality, she had a part-time job.

"Well, yeah, but...mmm...ehhh... I don't know about that."

I didn't want to be a gold digger, piggybacking off of my girlfriend's money, especially since I knew she would empty her entire bank account for me without batting a lash. *Seriously, girl, you're lucky I'm not that selfish.*

"But I don't have anything else to spend my money on."

Then keep saving it! You never know when you might actually need it! But of course, in *her* eyes, that time was right now.

"Hmmm... Then I guess I should get a part-time job myself."

"You're gonna get a job?"

"Yep!" I laughed. "Then we can both pay for the trip together. I'm like 99 percent sure it'll be more fun that way." Balance is key, as they say.

Adachi seemed to accept this; she nodded eagerly, her eyes sparkling. At the very least, I could see why she would prefer to travel with just me. And in that moment, she truly lit up the room.

But right as we were about to make a pinky promise, I belatedly realized that the Trio was staring at us. *Uh oh.* I'd totally forgotten they were there, so I'd been speaking at a normal volume this whole time. But the issue wasn't the noise level—judging from the looks on their faces, I could tell they sensed something was...*going on* between us.

"You two sure are close, aren't you?" Sancho asked, seemingly on behalf of the others. Her lips were curled in a stiff smile that was anything but affectionate; she pulled her legs in, close to her body. Meanwhile, the implication hung in the air.

"Uhhh...yeah, maybe," I replied evasively.

"We are," Adachi declared, grabbing my hand and erasing any ambiguity from my statement. I was so flummoxed, I kinda let it happen, and before I knew it, her grip was too tight for me to escape.

The Trio froze as Adachi raised our joined hands, practically rubbing it in their faces. My body burned hot. Then my ears started to ring and my head began to throb. There was no talking my way out of it.

"Uhhh, yeah!"

No, we're not—yeah, we are. It's not what it looks like— actually, it is. She's a good friend—a good girlfriend.

At this point, I decided I couldn't keep hiding it. Being considerate and cooperative was simply not in Adachi's wheelhouse. She wasn't predisposed to playing nice with others, and she probably didn't *want* to. Now that I was dating her, this was what life was going to be like.

Interpersonal relationships: complicated and fragile and intense and powerful, all at once. This, after the Trio went out of their way to invite us to their group... With a heavy heart, I rose to my feet and dragged Adachi from the room. I didn't have any set destination in mind, but I couldn't sit there for a single minute longer.

Granted, I had inadvertently left Yashiro behind, but she'd probably be fine. If the Trio went through my stuff and found her, well, I'd cross that bridge when I came to it.

As we walked down the hallway, my chest continued

to burn hot, and my brain boiled uselessly in my skull. Something akin to impatience swirled in my eyes.

"We *are* close, aren't we?" Adachi asked, seeking my confirmation. But our tightly linked hands left no room for debate.

"Yeah."

Adachi Sakura only knew one way of life: clumsily charging forward without giving any thought to the destruction she might cause in the process. But for right now, I was willing to give it a try.

So I laced my fingers with hers.

As time flowed like the sand in an hourglass, I bent down and scooped up a handful of sand. For better or for worse, it all glittered in my palm, so it was hard to pick out just the best bits. All I could really do was stare down at it and think. If I lumped all these memories together as a package deal, then overall, Adachi had changed my life for the better...you know, probably.

"Probably."

Adachi and I were eating in the dining hall with the rest of our group, though I could feel an invisible wall between us and them. It was my first time trying miso soup with carp dumplings, and since I'd never had the opportunity to eat carp before, I was curious to try them, but...to be completely honest, they were way too fishy for me. It was probably something I could theoretically get used to over time, but yeah... The miso really didn't do much to hide the smell.

To be fair, mass-produced food was never especially delicious. If I ordered it at a fancy restaurant, it'd probably be great. Not that I could picture myself wanting to do that.

I lifted my soup bowl to my lips and peered over the rim at the rest of the dining hall. The vermilion walls were illuminated a little too brightly, and the garish color stabbed my eyeballs. Vines were painted on the ceiling above us.

After my gaze wandered for a bit, I looked back at my meal, and the sounds around me came back into focus. When you stuffed a bunch of giddy high-schoolers into the same enclosed space, the resulting cacophony was on par with 5 o'clock traffic; I could feel the sound rising like bathwater, filling the room. But though I was sitting smack-dab in the middle of it, I felt divorced from it, almost like I was off sulking in the corner. I was supposed to be sitting with my "group" and yet, we were divided into a pair and a trio.

I felt like a crawfish in an irrigation ditch—okay, too obscure. It felt like... like Adachi and I were eating our dinner inside a glass box. But in most cases, the "walls" I felt were merely a product of my own mind. *I* was the one putting that distance between us. I was afraid that we had ruined our chances of getting along with the rest of our group.

We were failing to coexist peacefully, even in the smallest of communities. This was not a good thing. It would probably make our lives a lot harder going forward, and that made me sad. As for Adachi, however, she didn't look sorry in the least—she just kept eating her food in silence. She was so strong... Perhaps having too many pillars of support put you at risk anytime one of them crumbled.

In a different sense, Nagafuji was strong too—because she walked into the dining hall wearing one of the complimentary yukatas provided in each room. When the teachers yelled at her, she apologized deeply and promised to go change clothes...then turned and promptly sat down at the dinner table like the whole exchange never happened.

"I can't believe you," Hino muttered under her breath.

"What can I say? I'm the kind of girl who tries to se-quence-break the tutorial level," Nagafuji declared.

"...This is *the tutorial level* to you?"

In the end, maybe Nagafuji was the biggest rebel of us all.

"Hmmm..."

I contemplated bringing Yashiro the thin orange slices that came with my salad, even though it wasn't much. To be fair, she *did* say she didn't strictly need to eat, but... then why was she always stuffing her face back at our house? Was it more of a hobby? If so...I wasn't quite sure how to feel about that. As I reached out with my chop-sticks, however, my elbow collided with Adachi's.

"Ack! Sorry!" It wasn't the first time this had happened tonight, either. Only in times like these did I remember that she was left-handed. "I should probably try to sit on your right from now on, huh?"

"Probably," she nodded as she quietly dismantled her fried fish.

Once again, she showed literally no interest in her meal. Had she ever openly enjoyed eating something? I thought back over my memories of her, but nothing stood out to me. *The only thing she seems to take interest in is...me*, I realized bashfully.

Adachi was an innocent soul. No one had ever tried

to reach out to her—not even her own parents, oddly enough. So when I was the only person leaving grimy fingerprints all over her, part of me started to feel like maybe I should step back and keep her pristine instead. She was too precious for me to tarnish.

"Shimamura?"

My gaze must have wandered to her of its own accord, because she sounded confused. "How's your food?" I asked quickly.

"Uh, pretty so-so," she answered as she chewed the hard, undercooked rice. *Shocker.*

"Do you have any favorite foods? Sorry if I already asked this before, but I don't remember!" I asked in a light tone of voice. *Seriously, I wouldn't trust my own memory if you put a gun to my head.*

She started to say, "Not really," then fixed me with a suspicious look, silently asking me to explain myself.

"I just want to learn everything about you, one fact at a time." Maybe *this* was why I felt walled off—because I kept making cringey comments in public.

Then again, perhaps someone like Adachi felt right at home in this glass box, since it kept out all the potential threats. Her expression softened, and she began to mull it over. "Favorite foods... Water, I guess?"

"What are you, a plant?"

She chuckled and averted her eyes shyly. Then she looked back at me and countered with "What about you?"

"Oh, um...okonomiyaki?"

"Yeah, I know. What else?"

"Uhhh...tamagoyaki?"

I held up the bite of egg I was currently working on. Whoever cooked it had flavored it on the sweet side, which I liked. Adachi looked at my plate, picked up her chopsticks, and started to transfer all of her uneaten tamagoyaki to me.

"You don't have to do that, you know." *But I mean, if you want me to have them, I'm not complaining.*

And so dinner came to an end.

"What are you gonna do with those?" Adachi asked, pointing to the orange slices in my hands. It wasn't unreasonable for her to be curious, either, since I had once again asked to have hers in addition to my own. In fact, she gave me her whole salad, which I could have done without.

"Uhhh...don't worry about it." I couldn't possibly tell her that it was an offering to be made at the Altar of Yashiro, i.e., my backpack.

When we arrived back at our room, the rest of our group was nowhere to be seen. Adachi hovered near the entrance, glancing around like she didn't know where to sit. I looked over at my backpack sitting in the far corner of the room, making sure it wasn't wriggling on its own.

"Think the TV works?"

Unlike everything else in the room, which had all sort of faded and blurred together, the television was brand new. I could see the remote control on the floor nearby; Adachi rushed over, picked it up, and rushed back. *What are you, five? Cutie.*

"Let's test it out."

"Okie-doke."

At my prompting, she pressed the power button. Lazily, her gaze drifted to the TV screen, and I could tell at a glance that she couldn't care less about doing this. After a short pause, light and sound filled the room.

"Well, it's working... Any idea how to find the channels?"

"I dunno," she murmured as she fiddled with the remote.

Meanwhile, I walked over to the corner of the room and offered the thin orange slices to my backpack. They were vacuumed up in a matter of milliseconds. How could Yashiro tell what I was doing if she couldn't see me?

I willfully disregarded this disturbing question and substituted a different one:

"You're not making a mess in there, are you?" I whispered.

She popped up casually. "No need to worry."

Gah! Stay in there! It reminded me of a scene from that one animal documentary I was watching. *Was it the one about axolotls? No, what was it...? Oh, right, prairie dogs.*

"I engulf the food with my entire body when I eat, so there is no mess."

"Uhhhhh...okay." There was no point trying to understand it, so I just went with it. I figured I could trust her. As she started to retreat back into my backpack, however, a thought occurred to me: "Oh, right. Later, I'll sneak you into the bath with me."

Somehow I got the sense that it wouldn't be much of an issue. With Yashiro, it rarely ever was.

"I do not require a bath."

"Sure you do! You've been stuck in my backpack all day long! You need to stretch your legs." *Ugh, am I even hearing myself right now?*

"Hey, uh, Shimamura?"

"Wha?!" Startled, I whirled around and found myself draped in Adachi's shadow.

"You're talking to yourself a little too much today. You okay?"

Great, now my girlfriend's worried about my sanity. Once I confirmed that Yashiro was out of sight, I donned a smile. "I just like to hear myself talk, that's all." *Ugh, listen to me! I really need to start thinking before I speak!* Then again, I was lazy by nature, so perhaps that was a bit too optimistic.

"Well, y-you should talk to...to me instead."

Adachi knelt down beside me, and since she was so much taller than me, it was actually mildly intimidating. Well, until you factored in her meek, self-effacing attitude. Then it was just kind of funny.

"Bring it on, or whatever..."

Once again, her attempt at a joke was ruined by her poor delivery and beet-red face. And every time it happened, it was super adorable.

"Okay, then, what do you want to talk about?" I asked with a goofy grin.

On a whim, I reached out and touched her hair, combing her bangs away from her cheek. She flinched, then shyly placed her hand on mine, her fingers tracing my knuckles with all the grace of a trained harp player. She smiled, wide-eyed, which made for a funny-looking expression.

"That tickles."

But just then, the door opened and the Trio walked in. As soon as they spotted us, they stopped short at the entrance. We were caught. Cursing my carelessness, I pulled my hand away from Adachi—but in their eyes, it was perhaps all the confirmation they needed. The sound of the TV felt deafeningly loud. We had inadvertently given them the wrong idea. Except it wasn't the wrong idea at all.

With nothing to say for ourselves, we sat there without a word. A meaningful silence descended over the room as the Trio filed in and sat by the TV. The news was on, announcing tomorrow's weather forecast, but I was barely listening. Somewhere, I could hear the *tick-tock* of a clock drilling against the back of my neck.

There was still quite some time before our scheduled hot spring bathing period would begin. If this were any other group, we'd idle away the time talking, laughing, and having fun, but our group didn't have that kind of vibe. Adachi and I had cleaved a rift between us and them.

Sounds badass, I mused in spite of myself, but this was no time for ditzy jokes.

Adachi had clearly noticed the awkward tension but was choosing to remain silent, so all eyes were on *me* instead. But I couldn't risk the possibility that Adachi might tell them, like, *way* more than they needed to know. She was impossible to predict.

As the silence lingered, the air in the room grew heavier and heavier. There was no exchange of ideas to get things circulating again. But unlike me, Adachi didn't seem to feel uncomfortable in the slightest, so I would have to take matters into my own hands.

"Why don't we explore the inn a little?" I suggested, as a pretext to escape.

"Sure, but...I mean, is there anything worth seeing?"

Admittedly, now that we were all used to the smell of sulfur, it was really just an old, decrepit building. Nevertheless, I insisted. "Well, let's find out!"

While I was at it, I slung my backpack over my shoulder. After what just happened, I couldn't afford to make any more careless mistakes. Especially if it involved a certain blue-haired alien.

"We'll be back at bath time," I announced to no one in particular as I walked out.

"Have fun," Sancho replied in farewell, and I could tell from her tone that she wasn't sure how to interact with us. *Trust me, the feeling's mutual.*

After we left, would they all start gossiping about us?

The prospect made me depressed. I didn't want them talking smack about things that weren't true... Then again, if they talked smack about things that *were* true, that would suck worse, since I'd have no way of denying it.

"Now then, where to?" I pondered aloud. I didn't know the layout of this building, so we were in danger of getting lost.

"You brought your backpack?" Adachi commented, glancing at it.

"Oh, well, I thought I might want to buy something." *Yeah, let's go with that.*

We headed downstairs to the front lobby. Surprisingly, we didn't encounter any classmates loitering around; instead, we arrived right as a group from a different school was walking in. *Man, there really are a lot of schools doing field trips at this time of year,* I thought to myself as we sat down on a mahogany-colored bench. There was a souvenir shop located right nearby.

The gaps between the four provided benches were furnished with vases full of big yellow flowers. The positioning of said benches kinda reminded me of a hospital waiting room, but the lobby of an inn wasn't that different, right? Overhead, I could see a green-and-white fire exit sign flickering on and off at random intervals. As I looked up at it, I let out a breath. At last, I felt the relief that our private room should have offered me instead.

In a way, it was reminiscent of our days up in the gym loft—a moment of respite away from everyone else. It was how the two of us first met, so perhaps it was only natural that we found solace in it.

"I thought you said we were gonna explore," Adachi pointed out, confused, as she sat quietly beside me.

"I was planning to, but I changed my mind."

She laughed. "Are you for real?"

But she didn't seem to mind the speed at which I had seemingly changed my tune. She was probably just happy to have some alone time with me. *Not that we're actually alone, but she doesn't need to know that,* I thought to myself, glancing at my backpack.

"Adachi, are you..."

I waited for the rest of the question to come to me, but it never did. My mouth had simply decided not to finish what it had started.

"Am I what?"

"I don't know."

She looked at me in bafflement, and yeah, I couldn't really blame her. Believe it or not, she and I didn't talk all that much. We had spent so much time together, we didn't really *need* to.

"Wanna just zone out for a bit?" I suggested as a way to kill some time. With the lights on and Adachi next to me, I figured things would work themselves out.

"Sure," she murmured quietly. Then she faced forward, same as me. Together, we watched the other group of students as they waited at the front desk.

Then it occurred to me: with anybody else, this same silence would make me feel uncomfortable. But because I was with Adachi, I was at peace just sitting here, doing nothing. Perhaps this was proof of just how much I had come to trust her...though I didn't know exactly who, if anyone, I needed to prove anything to. Myself, maybe.

Alas, our alone time eventually came to an end. I checked my wristwatch, which I had chosen to carry in my pocket instead of on my arm. It was time to hit the hot springs.

I gestured to Adachi, and together we rose to our feet. All at once, her expression tensed. *I wonder what that's about,* I thought to myself as we started walking. Then, as we passed by the souvenir shop, I saw the snack buns they had out on display—the same kind you'd see in any grocery store. *Gee, what great souvenirs.*

"A jam-filled bun sounds lovely," my backpack muttered. I gave it a little smack for good measure.

My family never took trips to any hot springs, so I hadn't visited a public bath in a *loooong* time. Each class was assigned a certain time slot to use the facilities, but nevertheless, the women's changing room was packed. Girls stood at the sinks, wiping off their makeup; meanwhile, the teacher stood at the entrance, scolding anyone who was getting too rowdy. The lockers and walls were constructed with old wood that smelled faintly musty.

As I prepared to get undressed, I felt someone's eyes on me and quickly located the source. "Adachi?"

"It's nothing." She shook her head sharply as she reached for her bath towel. Her voice was as stiff as an undercooked potato.

She had been acting a bit strangely since well before we arrived. But I knew how much she struggled in social situations, so I could understand why she would feel anxious about taking a bath in a public setting. Unfortunately, there wasn't much I could do about it other than act as her moral support. In a way, she reminded me of the girls back in middle school who used to claim they were feeling sick so they wouldn't have to participate in a group activity they didn't like.

I pulled my shirt off, then slid out of my track pants, at which point I felt Adachi's gaze all over again. *"Aha!"* I exclaimed as I whipped my head around to look at her. Sure enough, she was looking at me. And she was already naked.

It was my first time seeing her in the nude, and my eyes automatically drifted to her long, slender legs. But before I could get a good look at her, she rushed off without me.

"Ada—"

"Nothing!" she cut in sharply as she tottered stiffly away.

"Hmmm..." *I sure hope she doesn't slip and fall.*

Once I had finished undressing, I followed after Adachi and walked face-first into the hot, muggy air. The humidity from the steam made my neck and eyebrows wet.

The main feature of the room was the rectangular sunken bathtub. The dim lighting was apparently intentional, warmly illuminating the wooden walls and ceiling. Additionally, there were three small windows, but I couldn't see much through the frosted glass. During the day, these windows probably let in sunlight and a hint of mountain greenery, but at night, they were just black squares.

Adachi was hidden among the other girls, sitting at a shower station. I couldn't see any bruises on her arms or legs, so I was relieved to learn that she hadn't slipped. But as I watched her, I noticed little oddities in her movements. She wasn't bending any of her joints. Even the simple act of turning the shower on required several steps at a slow, robotic pace. It reminded me of the way I felt whenever I'd get a neck cramp after sleeping. But of course, for Adachi, this wasn't all that uncommon.

"Is this seat taken?" I asked jokingly as I walked up to the station beside hers.

She flinched in surprise. "It's nothing!" She gestured for me to go ahead...but then her eyes widened. Clapping her hands to her cheeks, she hastily faced forward.

"Hmmm...?"

Confused, I watched as the water streamed onto her bright red cheeks... *Oh, well.* Now it was my turn to get the shower started. Like Adachi, I let the water stream down onto my face. Then I started aggressively wetting my hair.

As the pleasant warmth trickled down my body, I relaxed and let out a deep sigh of contentment. I could feel it slowly melting away all that built-up stress. To me, bath time signaled the end of a hard day, and I liked it very much.

Combing the wet strands of hair out of my face, I glanced nonchalantly around the room. *There she is!* I had waited for the perfect moment to set Yashiro free from my backpack, and now I could see her washing her hair at the farthest shower station. The shampoo suds had created a milky white afro on her head.

Naturally, the girl at the station next to her was staring at her in alarm, but she didn't seem to have the courage to actually say anything. Frankly, no matter what she said, Yashiro would answer with a cheerful smile, and the conversation would probably end there. Sure enough, as I watched, Yashiro noticed the girl looking at her and greeted her politely. Perplexed, the girl inclined her head in kind. *Yep, she'll be fine.*

"...Huh?" When I picked up the shampoo, I could feel a pair of eyes digging into my skin. I looked over and found Adachi frozen in place...so I summoned every last ounce of kindness and patience to the point that it probably seemed fake. "What's up, buttercup?"

"It's nothing," she shot back, averting her pointed gaze. Then she slapped her cheeks vigorously. *What is she so worked up about?*

"Hmmm..."

Every time I interacted with Adachi, she would react weirdly and tell me, "It's nothing," in a flat, emotionless voice. I mulled it over as I washed my hair and body. Then, once I was finished, I headed for the soaking tub. She dutifully tagged along with me.

"Awww, you waited for me? You didn't have to."

"It...it's nothing."

This was not a coherent response to my statement. At this point, I had to assume she wasn't processing a single word I said. Clearly her mind was elsewhere...but *where*?

Weaving our way through the other girls, we waded out to a spot against the wall and sat down in the water. It was so dim and damp, it kinda felt like we were in a cave somewhere, which was exciting. I was having a great time.

"Sure is fun to sit back and relax in a huge bathtub, huh?" I commented. When I was little, I used to be able to stretch my legs in the bathtub at home, too, but now I was too big for it. Growing up had its downsides.

I looked up at the pale steam clouds rising toward the wooden ceiling painted black, and for a while, I let myself pretend everything was fine.

"Now then..."

Without turning my head, I snuck a peek at Adachi next to me and met her gaze. She was blushing so hard, I half-expected her eyes to go all bloodshot, too.

"It's nothing," said the girl from Planet Nothing, her wet hair swaying as she shook her head.

"I didn't even say anything..."

Then she pressed her fingers into her closed eyes. No idea what that was about.

"Adachi, seriously, what's wrong?"

At this, she went full Crab Mode, sinking beneath the water's surface and blowing bubbles. *Not to be weird, but you probably shouldn't ingest public bathwater.*

"Hmmmm..."

I could detect the faintest hint of something I had suspected for a long time. For the time being, I faced forward...but I wasn't really seeing anything. Instead, all of my senses were focused on a particular area now outside my range of vision—the area where Adachi was located.

There it is.

After a moment, I could feel a different sort of heat mixed in with the rising steam: a heated gaze. It flickered away and back and away and back, almost like it was trying to send some kind of coded message.

"I see."

At this point, I couldn't keep playing dumb. It was looking like my suspicions were all but confirmed. Adachi was looking at me—ogling my body—and if I had to guess, probably because I was naked. She was my girlfriend, after all; she was in love with me. Of course, she would be attracted to me.

With this belated realization, I was in danger of veering into Crab Mode myself. But you know, if *crabs* could happily live their whole lives without any clothes... *Gah, now's not the time for jokes! This is about me and her—naked!*

"Well, um...uhhhhhh...ummm...*uhhhhhhhhh*..." I really wasn't sure if I should ask this question, but ultimately, my curiosity won out: "Do you like it?" *My naked body, I mean. Oh god, why did I ask?! What if she says yes?!*

Adachi was already flushed pink from the hot bathwater, but now she was burning scarlet with...you know... emotions and stuff. It was quite possibly the first time I'd ever seen her blush all the way to her forehead. She was so red, I half-expected her to pop like a balloon. *That can't be good for her blood pressure.*

"Whanothing!" she blurted, like she was inventing a new word. "It's nothing... It's nothing..." She hung her head, and her mouth drooped into the water as she mumbled, causing the surface to ripple and splash back up into her face.

For some reason I couldn't explain, this instilled in me a strange sense of duty: *I have to shake her out of Crab Mode or she'll suffocate to death.* "C'mon, I just want to talk about it... You can talk to me, can't you?" She had asked me to talk to her not too long ago, and now I was taking her up on it.

Crab Adachi straightened up slightly, returning to regular Red Adachi. Apparently, her time as a crab had boiled her brain. She looked at me, and her gaze started to drift south—but then she caught herself and pressed her hands to her eyes. *Good grief, she's so flustered.*

"I promise I won't get mad or weirded out, so tell me... do you like it?" Clearly, the heat had fried my senses too. Why on earth would we have this conversation in public?

She closed her eyes. I was expecting to get another "nothing," but evidently, she was still debating how to respond. Her panic created ripples in the water; I inadvertently found myself looking past them to what was scarcely concealed underneath.

Uh, yep. Growing up has its downsides, all right.

Once she was (comparatively) calm, she slowly opened her eyes, as if waking from a midday nap. Her eyes and lips were trembling so hard, part of me was afraid they might fall off of her face altogether. Then, in a tiny whimper, she said: "............Yes."

At last, the girl from Planet Nothing was speaking my language.

"So you like my body? Wow, ha ha..." Now *I* couldn't see straight. She had just confirmed that she liked seeing me naked.

"Uh, but to be clear, I don't mean it like *that*! I, uh— you're just so pretty that I—I mean, I can't help it? But not like *that*!"

"Okay, okay. Take it easy. Deep breath." If I let her keep babbling at me, we were liable to draw attention from everyone else in the room. "For now, let's not sweat the details about *why* you like it, 'kay?"

The second I started asking those kinds of questions, one or both of us would probably short-circuit and pass out in the tub. I could already feel steam shooting from my ears. Meanwhile, Adachi was stammering helplessly, her eyes damp with budding tears. If I didn't do something fast, she was headed straight back to Crab Mode.

Would she be offended if I asked her to keep her eyes to herself? If yes, then in what way? Could I play it off as a joke, like "Oh, my gosh, Sakura-san, you naughty girl"?

I mean, I probably *could*, but there was no telling if it would improve the situation. Manga was full of similar hot spring situations, but in all the series I'd read, I couldn't remember how any of the characters handled it.

At this point, I was tempted to lean into it and just let her look. Not like it would hurt anything...other than my dignity...or maybe her composure... *Okay, then, I guess it's fine. Wait, really?*

With my head perpetually in the sand, I couldn't see any problems at all.

"Well, uh...Adachi-san?"

Moments ago, I was relishing the ability to lounge with my legs stretched out, but now, suddenly, I felt compelled to sit up straight. As for Adachi, she looked like a clam with her shoulders hunched up around her ears.

"*Yeee?!*"

When she tried to speak, her voice cracked. She was in no condition to have a conversation. Thus, I decided to cut to the chase:

"Could you make it a little more...subtle? Like so I won't notice?"

It was the best compromise I could offer her.

"*Huh?!*"

She stared at me in disbelief, but I turned away as if the conversation was over. Then, instead of crossing my arms over my chest, I purposely held them down at my sides, pressing my palms to the bottom of the tub. I desperately wanted to give the impression that I wasn't bothered.

As I faced forward, I could see a whole bunch of naked classmates—no surprise there. I could also see a much smaller naked figure; somehow she had talked the girl next to her into washing her hair for her. Perhaps she was naturally imbued with the power to make others want to take care of her. But I digress.

My point is, there was a ton of nudity going on in here. Even *I* was naked. One would think it would have lost its novelty by now. But in Adachi's case, evidently not.

If I stopped dancing around this issue and actually started to probe into it, maybe I'd learn more about who she was as a person. It felt like I'd missed my chance to expound upon our unique connection. But this really didn't feel like the right time or place to delve into it. What we needed—*oh, god, she's looking! She's totally looking!*

Even with my gaze pointed in a completely different direction, it was *super* obvious. Not only that, but I could somehow *feel* exactly which parts she was focused on. If this was her idea of subtle, well, it needed some work.

Unable to stand it any longer, I turned and looked straight into her eyes.

"Wait...c-could you tell?!" She looked back at me in shock. *Are you kidding me?*

"Uhhh, nope! Had no idea!" A cold sweat trickled down my back as I prayed for her to believe my blatant lie.

"Oh, okay," she replied, relieved.

I could tell she wasn't messing with me—most likely, she was dead serious. About looking at my...uh...*areas*. Why was she staring so intensely? If I had to guess...she was probably holding herself back from going any further. *But I mean, if she's only gonna look, then there's nothing I need to worry about...right?*

As I sat there in the bath, I keenly felt my skin grow damp with sweat instead of water. Beside me was my same-sex partner, staring at my naked body. And I was letting her look. All the while surrounded by our classmates.

"Maybe this is a really bad idea..."

I had no cover story for any of it. Honestly, I was tempted to just stop thinking altogether. It felt like we were breaking the rules of the trip somehow.

Originally, I wasn't planning to stay for long, but in the end, we stayed in the tub until the very end of our scheduled timeslot. As for Adachi, she remained dizzy and flustered long after we had toweled off and gotten dressed, but was that because of the heat, or...something else?

For now, I would have to put that question on the backburner, because the answer was liable to cause a thousand more problems.

When I returned to our assigned room with my hair in a towel, I stepped in something cold and looked down at the floor. There was a trail of water leading toward my backpack like the fuse of a bomb. *Ugh, PLEASE dry yourself off before you climb inside my backpack!* Had she gotten my clothes or itinerary all wet? I was tempted to confront her, but couldn't risk her popping her head out. As I debated it, I casually brushed the water trail with my foot as I walked, wiping it up.

Then I approached my backpack and held out my dirty clothes. She promptly vacuumed them up. *Just don't eat them and we're cool.*

After that, the Trio came in and sat down on the opposite side of the room, ever so slightly keeping their distance from us. But while *they* were talking and laughing, the two of us remained silent. Adachi was sitting cross-legged with a towel over her head, still blushing, and I didn't know what to say to her. Not like we could joke about how she ogled my naked body for hours.

Would we get that comfortable with each other someday? I zoned out, trying to picture it, but with limited success. All I achieved was a small amount of embarrassment as my flushed skin gradually cooled off. Then, around the time my hair was finally dry, we all started rolling out our futons.

"Hmmmm." The Trio's beds seemed awfully far away from ours...or was I just getting paranoid?

"I'm pretty tired. Let's get some sleep," I heard one of them say.

Fair enough, I thought. The mood in the room wasn't exactly conducive to late-night gossiping, anyway. I wondered if the other groups were having more fun than we were... Some people seemed to have a knack for making friends with just about anybody. Like Hino and Nagafuji, for instance.

"Let's call it a night, or whatever!" said DeLos, though I wasn't sure what the "or whatever" was supposed to mean.

"Point taken." My body felt heavy, perhaps waterlogged from that intense bath.

As for Adachi, she was still zoned out, her body burning hot. I kinda wanted to ask her what she was thinking about, but another part of me was a little scared to find out. Our eyes met, and her bottom lip started to quaver. Then she shook her head vigorously—in response to what, I wasn't sure.

When I crawled into bed, I found the pillow stiff, and the fabric of the blanket felt different from the one I used at home. All of this served to put a spotlight on the fact that I was sleeping somewhere else tonight. The corners of the futon were damp and smelled of mold, but in a way, the temperature difference I felt against my toes was actually sort of soothing. Even though it didn't resemble my grandparents' futons, it instilled me with a similar feeling of homesickness.

"Lights out!" called Sancho (or was it Panchos?) as darkness descended over us.

For a while, I wasn't sure whether my eyes were open or shut; there was no longer any difference. But once my vision adapted, I caught a glimpse of Adachi's eyes shifting in the dark. She was looking at me with a level of composure that suggested she had overcome her embarrassment, and somehow, I could tell she was begging me to talk about something. I pressed a finger to my lips, reminding her that it was bedtime and other people were around.

She blinked at me rapidly, then extended her left hand out from under her futon...in my direction, naturally. Now it sat in the gap between our beds on the floor... After a moment, I belatedly realized what she wanted. Then I reached out in kind.

There, surrounded by perfect silence, Adachi and I held hands. Hers carried the lingering warmth of the hot spring water. Then I saw her expression soften and wondered if she was thinking the same thing about me.

But if we didn't scoot our futons closer, the others might see. No one was snoring yet, and if we fell asleep before they did, I was scared they might catch us.

What was it about Adachi's warmth that made me so drowsy? The only skin contact was through our palms, and yet it seemed to spread all the way to my chest. I could feel my reservations being dragged away on the tide.

Eh, whatever.

If the Trio weren't planning to get along with us, then I figured I may as well focus my energy on Adachi instead. Was it the right choice? That was for Future Me to decide, because right now, I didn't care. Future Me could use a little homework anyway.

At last, the first day of the school trip was coming to an end. Absently, I wondered if this was what it was *supposed* to be like...but on second thought, there was no single "correct" way to go on a field trip.

So in that sense, perhaps this was simply the Shimamura way.

interlude **Hino and nagafuji**

"**A**REN'T YOU BORED, Hino?"

As I sat at the shower station, washing my hair, I could hear the splash of a different water source behind me. I looked over my shoulder.

The bathtub at my house was rectangular in shape, constructed of umbrella pine, and took up an entire wall. According to Nagafuji, the tub alone was the size of her family's entire bathroom. She was floating on her stomach with her arms folded on the rim, her butt fully exposed, kicking her feet in the water.

"Bored of what?" I asked.

"Well, you know...day in, day out..."

Nagafuji gazed around the room at the walls and ceiling, contemplating her next words. She had been in the tub for so long, her whole body was pink, all the way to her ears. *I wish you'd spend this much time scrubbing yourself first.* Not only that, but the longer she stayed in the tub, the more incoherent she became. I tried to guess at what she could possibly be talking about, but couldn't think of anything.

"Look, you need to explain your entire thought process when you ask me these things." I dumped a pail of warm water over my head, then continued, "But it's also really tiring to listen to you blather on and on, so don't explain *too* much, got it?"

"You're so demanding, Hino!"

I debated whether to fling my pail at her.

"Gosh, where do I begin...?" Murmuring, she rested her cheek against the rim of the tub. She certainly *looked* like she was trying to think, but whatever it was, I knew it couldn't be that complicated. This was Nagafuji we were talking about.

I set my pail down and went back to scrubbing, starting from the arms. When I paused to think about it, I realized I always cleaned myself in a specific order. Did Nagafuji do it in order too? I must have seen it for myself not long ago, so I tried to remember.

"I was thinking...it must be boring, washing yourself in this huge bathroom all alone every day," she concluded at last. *See? I knew it wasn't complicated.*

"That's it?"

"Yeah."

Why did she take so long to think of that? And what did she mean by "bored"? I tilted my head, and my wet hair clung to my face and neck. "No, I can't say I've ever been *bored* in the bathroom."

"Then what kinda stuff do you think about?"

"Nothing much. I just sorta space out and think about the last manga I read."

"Your brain is a muscle. Use it or lose it!"

"Great advice, dippy. *You* should try it sometime."

It was baffling to me that she managed to get such good grades. Did she honestly use her brain more than I did?

"Well, what are you thinking about right now?"

"I'm thinking, 'Wow, someone sure is splashing *really loud* in here.'"

She kept kicking the water with both feet, over and over and over. In fact, she didn't seem to realize she was doing it until I pointed it out. "Oh, that?" She looked at her nails, which were as pink as the rest of her. "My feet wanted to help alleviate your boredom!"

"Well, it's annoying, so tell 'em to knock it off."

I gave the soles of my feet one last scrub. Then, after

I rinsed myself off, I finally headed for the tub. It was so roomy, even Nagafuji's huge bazonkers couldn't fill it up—so why, with all this space, did I feel the need to jump in right next to her? As I submerged myself up to my shoulders, I looked at the wall and chuckled. "Maybe I don't use my brain after all."

At a distance, the space next to Nagafuji looked so *empty*. I was compelled to fill it purely on instinct.

"You know, I really like your bathtub, Hino."

"Do you?"

"Yeah. And I really like you too."

"What am I, an afterthought?" *Kind of a crappy way to confess your love, but sure.*

Her legs and butt bobbed up and down. "That reminds me, Hino."

"What is it now?"

She fell silent, staring straight ahead. *Splash, splash, splash.*

After a long moment, I repeated my question. "What is it?"

"I forgot what I was going to say."

"...Figures."

For a while I sat there, boiling in the water with Nagafuji. Then, when I reached my limit, I rose to my feet.

"I'm getting out."

"Did you make sure to count to 10,000?"

"Yeah, totally," I lied as I stepped out. For whatever reason, she tagged along with me.

It was the night before the school trip, and Nagafuji had come to sleep over at my house "because we'll be busy tomorrow." As if that made any sense.

"Freshly poached Hino!" she exclaimed as she pinched my bicep. Water dripped from her hair and onto me.

"Quit touching me and go towel off, would ya?"

"Oops."

She whipped her hair back, sending more droplets flying into my face as the strands slashed at my nose and forehead. *Good grief.* Scowling, I stood next to her and set about drying myself off. With the two of us, the changing room was a little cramped.

"For that matter, why do you always wanna join me in the bath, anyway?"

Surely, most people would take the hint.

"Huh? Because it's fun!"

"...You really haven't changed since we were kids, have you?" *Except for your boobs.*

"Well, a bathroom this huge is kinda wasted on a single person, don'tcha think?"

"It's supposed to feel *luxurious*, birdbrain." *You have weird priorities.*

Then, after we had changed into our PJs...

"Pretty bland, isn't it?" she remarked.

"Huh?"

"Oh, I mean the food here," she added, having learned her lesson from earlier.

"Ah, yeah. They all seem to like it that way."

Nothing but plain food for every meal. This was one of many "traditions" that my family was obsessed with, and my parents and brothers all made sure there were *never* any deviations. For better or for worse, our culture dictated that we close ourselves off to the outside world.

"Who cooks it, anyway? Your mom?"

"The help." My mother only ever entered the kitchen to make tea. Hell, half the time, she wasn't even here.

As Nagafuji dried her hair, the slightest motions made her chest jiggle beneath her shirt. *Good grief, what has humanity come to? Take that!* I pushed them up for added support. In retaliation, she flicked me in the head, then continued, "Whenever I eat that stuff, it never really feels like I've eaten anything."

"Yeah, same."

"Therefore, I demand a snack before bed."

"Who died and made you queen?"

Nevertheless, we left the changing room and headed for the kitchen. Surely, we could find a little something to nibble on.

When I walked in, it smelled like radishes—prep for tomorrow's dinner, maybe. A maid was standing at the stove, tending to the pot. She promptly noticed me. "How can I help you?"

"Oh, I'm just swinging by for a sec," I told her as I scanned the cabinets and countertops. When I spotted what I was looking for, I snatched it up and hurried out. No need for freshly brewed tea when we still had some back in my room.

Out in the hall, I showed Nagafuji the spoils of my battle.

"Found us some star candies."

"Ooh, nice."

They were the same kind I'd seen in passing when I went to pick up our order at the local tea shop. Incidentally, the daughter of the family who ran the place was *also* endowed with a huge rack. *Humanity's doomed at this rate.*

Together, we returned to my room, where Nagafuji's futon had been laid out. We had guest rooms too, of course, but in my eyes, she was hardly a *guest*... Why did I keep thinking about Nagafuji so much? Clearly, my brain was still fuzzy from the heat. "What flavor do you want?"

"Red."

"I said *flavor*, genius!" I hissed as I pinched her cheek. After the long bath, this freshly poached Nagafuji was practically glistening.

"They're all just sugar-flavored, aren't they?"

"These are different," I insisted. Then I set the four tins down on the floor so she could see them.

"Coffee, black tea, green tea, and...*roasted* green tea...?"

She cocked her head in confusion. If I had to guess, she was expecting something very different. Alas, no cute pastel colors here—just muddy browns and greens.

"Why are they all coffee- and tea-flavored?"

"Because that's what my family likes."

She scrutinized each of the tins in turn, then picked up the green tea and pulled the lid off with an audible *shpop*. "Oh, that's a fun sound." Then she closed it again.

"What are you doing?"

Shpop, shpop, shpop.

"Enough! Just have some already!"

"Grrrr..."

Reluctantly, she set the lid down. *How do you always*

manage to get distracted by every little thing? Then she plucked up one of the star candies, its verdant green color enhanced by her flushed red fingers, and popped it into her mouth. As she crunched it between her molars, her eyes widened.

"Mmmm?" She took a second, then a third, and after she swallowed them, she exclaimed with glee, "These are really good!"

"The best money can buy," I snarked.

"No kidding."

After that, she started snacking with gusto. *Easily impressed, this one.* Meanwhile, I took a sip of my bottled tea, though it had gone lukewarm after hours away from the fridge. "Want some?" I offered.

"Sure."

I handed it to her, and she took a sip. There was a pause.

"Wait, what the?" She blinked back at me. "Aren't you going to have some candy?"

"Nah, I'm good. Too lazy to go brush my teeth again afterward."

"Want me to brush them for you?"

For a moment, I pictured it...

"Don't be stupid."

"Well, now I feel guilty sitting here, eating your candy without you!"

Or so she claimed, but she sure didn't *look* very guilty with that smile on her face. At this rate, she might just empty every last tin... Quietly, I withdrew the other flavors to safety, lest my parents complain.

"Are you excited for the school trip?" she asked.

"Yeah, I guess," I shrugged.

"Ever been to the Kyushu region before?"

"Nope! My folks hardly ever stay in Japan for their vacations. Nothing worth seeing, according to them."

"Oh."

That's all you have to say? Do you care more about the candy than your question?

"Where did you guys end up going for your last vacay?"

"Hawaii, remember? I bought you souvenirs and everything!"

"What about before that?"

"Italy! Ditto on the souvenirs!"

"And the time before that?"

"Now look here, you..."

Knowing her, she would keep on asking until I ran out of answers, so I decided to nip it in the bud. She gazed back at me, star candies pinched between her fingers.

"If you pride yourself on knowing every last thing about me, then try to memorize this stuff on your own!" *And you had the nerve to tell ME to use MY brain!*

I didn't think what I said was that terribly shocking, and yet she froze, startled, like I'd just hit her with a huge revelation. Then, at last, a derpy smile spread on her face. "Yeah, you're right."

"Damn right I'm right!"

"Yep, yep!" She nodded, beaming. Finally, it felt like I'd proven myself more important than some stupid overpriced candy. Then she reached out, carrying the glittering sugar crystals between her fingers. "You're so cute, Hino."

"Wha—stop that!"

"Maybe I should touch *your* boobs for a change."

"Knock it off, you Neanderthal!"

First we ate dinner together, then took a bath together, and now it was time to talk about random stuff until we fell asleep... Perhaps for us, the school trip had already begun.

WHEN I GET HOME from school, I spot Yachi hunched over, sitting in the middle of the hallway for some reason. What is she doing? I kick my shoes off and walk up to her, but she doesn't even notice my shadow approaching. I give her butterfly hair a little tug.

"Mmm?" She looks up. "Well, if it isn't Little."

Now I can see what's in her lap. "Is that an encyclopedia?" There's a bunch of pretty birds on the cover, including one I recognize: a parakeet.

"Shimamura-san allowed me to borrow it."

"Oh, you're right! That's from the bookshelf in our room!"

Dad bought us a whole set. There's one about fish, one about reptiles, and one about bugs too. My sister really hates that one.

"I am still woefully ignorant about Planet Earth, you see," she says with her usual smug chuckle. I hope the encyclopedia tells her it's not normal to have blue hair.

"Why are you sitting out here in the hallway?"

"It makes no difference where I sit," she answers flatly. I guess that's true. She has a weird outlook on a lot of things, but it doesn't make her wrong about any of it, per se.

Yachi goes back to staring at the encyclopedia—real intensely, almost like a statue. The only part of her that moves is her wispy butterfly hair. On a whim, I stick my finger in her loopy-loops. "Are you having fun?"

She doesn't reply.

"Do you like birds?"

"I am studying."

She sounds kinda...annoyed at me. "Grrrr." She's no fun.

Should I drop my backpack off in our room? Nah. I walk straight to the kitchen, where I find my mom refilling the pepper shaker. There's a bunch of grocery bags everywhere, so I guess she just got back from shopping.

"I'm back, Mom."

"Cool. Welcome home."

"Can I have a sweet snack?"

She turns to look at me, then scans the shelves. "Something *sweet*, huh? All right, hold out your hands."

I do as she tells me. What's she gonna give me?

"I said *hands*, plural," she insists.

I hold out my other hand, too. Whatever it is, I guess she's gonna give me a lot.

"Here you go."

Without a sound, my palms turn white.

"Is this just...sugar?"

"Well, you said *something sweet*, right?"

Grinning, she licks the sugar from her fingers. This is all I get? I stare down at my palms.

"Is she gonna like it...? I don't know..." Disappointed, I head back the way I came. Then, when I return to Yachi's spot in the hallway, I call out to her: "Yachi! I brought you some sugar!"

...Will it work?

"Yay!"

It worked. I can't believe it. Yachi dives face-first into my palms and vigorously licks them up and down. Her chilly tongue slides between my fingers—it tickles! She vacuums up every last speck of sugar. Now her mouth and chin are *covered* in it.

"Look at what a mess you've made!"

I set down my backpack and pull out a pack of tissues. But as I'm wiping Yachi's mouth, Nee-chan walks out from our room with two packed bags. She drops them off by the front door.

"Oh, hey, welcome home," she says when she sees me, followed by "Oh, wait, one more thing... No, two more things!" Then she runs back to our room. She's in a rush.

"Nee-chan's going on a school trip tomorrow," I explain to Yachi.

"I see, I see."

Somehow Yachi can juggle eating sugar, reading the encyclopedia, and talking to me, all at the same time. Her eyes and ears and mouth are all doing different things... Well, I guess that's normal. But in Yachi's case, it feels like they aren't really connected.

"Have you ever been on a trip, Yachi?" Oh, wait—her being here is probably the same thing as a trip.

"I believe this counts as one."

"Right..."

"You see, I hail from far in the west." She points at the wall on the left side. Is that where the west is?

"How far is far?" I ask.

"On foot, it would take you seven million years to get there."

"...Oh." I can't picture it at all. "If I went there, would there be others like you?"

"There are others like me all around us as we speak."

"No there's not!"

"Would you like to study with me, Little?" She picks up the encyclopedia and offers it to me.

"Ummm...okay." Feels like anything's fun as long as we're together. "But just so you know, I like fish better than birds."

"I see," she replies. "Just a moment." She takes the encyclopedia and dashes off to our room. After a little while, she comes back, carrying a different encyclopedia with a cover that's bluer. "I have exchanged the books."

"How very thoughtful of you," I say, mimicking the way she talks. Oops! It tends to slip out if I'm not careful.

She sits back down in the middle of the hallway and opens the book. I try to peer over her shoulder, but no luck.

"I can't see, Yachi!"

"Oh, dear." Right as I try to lean around her from the side, she jumps to her feet. "In that case, why don't you sit here, Little?"

She pushes me into the spot where she just was, and I tumble into it. At first I think it won't change anything, but then she leans her weight against my back, and her sparklies rain down on me. She's always cold to the touch.

"Now then, let us begin our studies."

"Yachi, can you see from there?"

"Not to worry. I don't need my eyes to see."

"...What?" I look over my shoulder at her.

She points at her eyes with her fingers. "I only made these in order to blend in with other Earthlings. They move, but they otherwise have no function. Ha ha ha ha ha!"

I don't get it. She's telling me the eyes I'm looking at don't actually work? But they're looking right at me, and they're wet, and they're blinking... I just don't get it!

"Then how do you *see*?" How do you see the encyclopedia, or the sugar, or me?

"With this!" Beaming, she taps lightly on her skull.

"With...your brain...?"

"Yes."

She barely explained anything, but I guess that's all I'm gonna get. Now I can't even focus on studying.

Yachi's mysteries extend beyond just her looks. The longer I think about it, the deeper down the rabbit hole it goes—and the scarier it gets. But one look at that sunny smile and everyone seems to forget.

Something tells me this adorable creature resting against my back can't be found in any encyclopedia on Earth.

3. Our First Trip
PART 2

FOR ONCE IN MY LIFE, I awoke with my brain fully functional. Normally, my mornings were spent in a soporific haze that liked to linger for as long as possible, but this time, everything was sharp and clear. I stared up at the ceiling for a minute, then looked over at my right hand extending out from under my blanket. Generally speaking, I tossed and turned a lot in my sleep (or so my family always told me), and at some point, I had pulled away from Adachi. But my palm was warm, as if we were still connected in spirit.

I pushed the blanket off and sat upright in the dim light of dawn. First, I looked over at my backpack in the corner; next, I checked the time on the clock on the wall; then, finally, I looked at Adachi. She was sound asleep with her entire body facing me. I could hear rhythmic breathing from all the other futons too.

I contemplated going back to sleep myself, but there *was* a certain something I needed to take care of while no one was looking. Shaking off the temptation of my warm bed, I rose to my feet. Then, I grabbed my backpack and carefully slipped out of the room.

Out in the hall, my feet sank into the plush carpet, muffling the noise. Unable to detect any signs of life, I headed downstairs to the lobby. Fortunately, the souvenir shop was already open for business. I greeted the bored-looking cashier and bought a jam-filled bun. *Gee, how exciting,* I snarked to myself. Then, I spotted a vending machine farther down the hall. Once I had concealed myself in its shadow, I crouched down, slid my backpack to the floor, and offered it breakfast.

"You awake?"

"Good morning, Shimamura-san." Yashiro popped her head out, and her eyes lit up with excitement. "Wow!"

"Here's your breakfast."

"Ooooh!"

She took the package and gleefully unwrapped it, all the while too lazy to get out of my backpack. Then she began to chow down with the voracity of a garbage disposal.

"Does it taste like destiny?"

"It does indeed."

Glad to hear it. Just make sure you finish it before anyone sees you. Honestly, I still couldn't believe that she was actually here with me...and with both of us gone, my kid sister was all alone back at home...

"Sure hope she's not lonely without us."

"I should have invited her to join me in your backpack."

"As if!" *My sister's not an unidentified life-form like you, thank you very much.*

After Yashiro had finished wolfing down her bun, I used a tissue to wipe her mouth. "I appreciate it," she told me. Personally, I just didn't want her getting crumbs in my backpack. Once I was finished, her hand shot eagerly into the air. "Really! I am truly grateful to you, Shimamura-san!" And with that, she disappeared into the backpack like a small woodland creature retreating into its den. That was all I got from her—just *gratitude*.

"Ha ha ha..."

But on the other hand, perhaps gratitude was the purest human emotion there was. After all, when you were grateful, it meant you got something in return. But of course, Yashiro wasn't the calculating type.

"Now, then..."

I picked up my backpack. Was this how those delinquent anime characters felt whenever they fed a stray cat out behind the school building? Come to think of it, Adachi and I were both categorized as delinquents just last year. *Cat-egorized. Heh.*

But right as I started to head back to our assigned room, I heard a gasp. Casually shifting my backpack behind me, I looked over.

"Sup!"

"Oh, hey. Good morning." I blinked. It was Panchos.

Unlike Sancho, she had long hair; right now, that hair was unbrushed, and her bangs were pinned up, revealing her large forehead. The tracksuit she wore in place of PJs wasn't very tidy either. The hems of her pants were so low, they were trailing on the floor, and the heels of her shoes were smashed flat.

I wasn't expecting to see her here, but I *really* wasn't expecting her to say hi to me.

"You're sure up early."

"You too."

As far as I could tell, she was awake, but only just. She came to a stop in front of the vending machine, scanned the options, and pressed one of the buttons. Then, she realized she hadn't put any money in.

"Oops... Well, this is embarrassing." Laughing, she pulled out her wallet. "I just came to get a drink, so I wasn't expecting to bump into anybody. Especially not this early!" She rubbed her sleepy eyes.

"I feel you," I agreed curtly.

Once she had fed her money into the machine, she hit the button twice, and two bottles of tea dropped down. Then, after she retrieved her change from the tray, she offered me one of the bottles. "Here."

"...Thanks." But why would she buy one for me?

She walked up next to me, uncapped her drink, chugged it, and let out a sigh of relief as she stared absently at the far wall. I crouched down and set my backpack in between us, but she remained standing... Was she planning to hang out for a while? I started to twist the cap off my own drink, stopped, started again, then stopped again. Meanwhile, it was Panchos who broke the silence.

"Hey, so...are you and Adachi-san, like...a thing?"

I was *not* expecting her to go there. I stayed quiet at first, unsure how to react. But she seemed to have anticipated this, because she continued.

"Oh, I don't mean it in a rude way or anything. I won't tell anyone!" She rolled up her sleeve and flexed her bicep.

"Whoa, check out those guns," I joked.

"Yeah, I work out."

I wasn't sure how her fitness level was supposed to convey trustworthiness, but whatever. It took serious dedication to build up that kind of muscle, so maybe that was what she was offering. "Well, to answer your question...yeah, you could say we're a thing," I told her.

"Hmm," she replied, every bit as evasive as my statement had been. She averted her gaze, then continued. "So you guys are going steady?"

"What are you, 80?" Someone our age would *never* use slang that ancient.

"No way! I'm hip and with it!" she protested. "I play, uh, Tsum Tsum! All the time!"

"Oh, really?"

It was clear to me that she had only ever heard the name. Likewise, I'd never played it either. And for that matter, I wasn't sure it was trendy anymore.

"Interesting. Well, then."

"If you don't have anything to say, you don't have to force yourself."

"Oh, okay. Thanks."

She smiled softly, closed her eyes...then immediately opened them again and looked at me.

"So you're going steady?" she repeated.

"Yeah, I guess we are." Adachi asked me to be her girl-friend, and I agreed to it. Pretty steady if you asked me.

"I gotta say, you're the first bona fide couple I've seen at our school."

"Same-sex couple?"

"No, no, I mean... Obviously, I've heard rumors about people at school dating each other, but it's always so hush-hush. I've never seen it with my own eyes, y'know? Or been a part of it..." She blushed faintly, be it her own lack of experience, or maybe she had unrequited feelings for someone at school.

"Yeah, I feel you." I twisted the lid off my bottle of tea. "Thanks for this, by the way," I added before taking a sip. The label said "light," so evidently this was what light tasted like. It was good.

"Soooo is this a hint?" she asked.

"What?"

"Are we intruding on you guys?" She bent her knees slightly as she looked at me.

"*Intruding*? I don't see it that way at all."

"Okay, but...I mean, I figure you probably want some alone time in the room..."

"To do what?"

"Oh, my god." She clapped both hands over her face, then peeked at me through the gaps in her fingers. "You *know* what I'm talking about!"

"I really don't!"

"*Kissy stuff*!"

"We wouldn't do kissy stuff on a school trip."

"So you admit to doing kissy stuff, like, somewhere else?" she pressed curiously.

Have we? I thought back over my memories. *Well, there was that one time I kissed her on the forehead... I guess that counts.* "Our relationship is still pretty love-letter tier, if you know what I mean."

"Love letters?" she repeated, sincerely puzzled.

How have you not heard about love letters? "You know, like pen pals?"

"Pals? So you're just gal pals?"

"Okay, then, pen girlfriends."

"Now you're just making stuff up!"

She giggled at me; I averted my eyes and smiled to myself. This was turning into a pretty fun conversation. Panchos was still a little fidgety, but at least she was smiling.

"So what sorta stuff do you do with Adachi-san?"

"I don't know... Normal stuff, I guess?"

"Okay, well, what 'normal stuff' do people do when they're in a relationship?"

"Beats me. It'd be a lot easier if they made a how-to guide." This was something I honestly struggled with. How were romantic relationships supposed to function?

As her mouth hung open, she reached up and pushed it shut. "I guess you don't know much more than I do, huh?" Unsurprisingly, she didn't have the answers either. "Well, where do you go on dates? You *do* go on dates, right?"

"I don't know if they count as dates, per se, but we go to the mall and stuff."

"That's the same thing I do with *them*!" she exclaimed, jerking her head in the vague direction of Sancho and DeLos.

"Yep," I nodded casually.

"And that counts as a date?"

"I think so," I shrugged.

"Okay," she nodded casually, but she didn't sound that convinced. "Wait—oh, my god, I just realized something."

"What?"

She leaned forward with a smirk. "I bet Adachi-san gets all dolled up for your dates while *you* just throw on whatever's clean!"

"What? I don't..." I started to protest, but paused to consider it. *Oh. Hmm.* "Okay, I guess I can see that... Ha ha ha ha..."

Laughing dryly, I looked away. This was something I never stopped to think about before now. *Maybe I should try a little harder next time. She's my girlfriend, after all... and I'm hers.*

"Y'know, Shimamura-san, after talking to you today, I can tell you're actually kind of a hot mess."

"I am?"

My mother always said that about me too, especially first thing in the morning when I had only just woken up. I wished I could get a glimpse of it, but by the time I had the energy to stagger to the bathroom mirror, there was no trace left—I was usually awake by then. But of course, that wasn't what Panchos was talking about.

There was a lull as the two of us sipped our drinks. If she wasn't here, I would have let Yashiro have some too. We were still the only people in the hall, and the only sound was the low hum of the vending machine.

"Can I ask you a kinda personal question?"

I shot her a look that said, *Another one?* She pressed the lid of her drink against her bottom lip.

"I don't want you to get mad, but I don't get a lot of

opportunities to ask about this stuff, so I'm curious. Not like you see it every day, right?"

"You don't?"

"Huh? You *do*?"

I thought about Hino and Nagafuji. "Well, I dunno. Maybe."

"Exactly! You never know for sure! That's why I wanna ask!" she explained eagerly.

"Well, I might not have an answer for you, but go ahead."

Satisfied with this, she grinned. "So...you're a lesbian?"

"Uhhhhh..."

One question in and I was already drawing a blank. Was I? I didn't exactly have much experience falling in love over the years.

"When you see the other girls in class, are you like 'Hoohoo, hottie!' and stuff?"

"*Hoohoo, hottie*?" I repeated, annoyed. Then I stared at her for a few moments. "No, I don't think so."

"Awww, were you checking me out? I'm flattered!" She beamed and scratched her cheek bashfully. "What about Adachi-san?"

"I don't know if she's a lesbian, but she's definitely in love with me."

In response, Panchos let out a wolf whistle.

"I mean, she only seems to have eyes for me," I clarified.

She whistled again, but this time it petered out and she started coughing. "God, that's *sooo* lovey-dovey!"

"Ha ha ha..."

She sounded pretty happy about it, at least.

Can't have "lovey-dovey" without a lovey and a dovey... I wonder which one I am.

"Okay, so expanding on my last question..."

"Yes?"

"When you see a girl's boobs, do you wanna squeeze—I mean, touch them?"

If you're going to rephrase it, at least stop squeezing the air with your hands. "Not really," I replied. "But if I see somebody with big boobs, I *do* tend to notice."

A common experience, if I had to guess. Was there anyone in the world who didn't notice that about Nagafuji, for instance?

"Gotcha. Well, would you say you look at them pretty often? *Hmm?*" With a jaunty hand on her hip, she thrust her chest out. She was about as well-endowed as Adachi, and if I wanted, I could totally cop a feel...

"Are you daring me to touch them or what?" I asked, knowing full well that the world wasn't that straightforward. Otherwise, we could live our whole lives like it's Didney Worl.

"Wha?!" Intimidated, Panchos moved to conceal her chest. "I mean, you *are* pretty cute... I guess if it was just once, but... Gosh, I didn't know you were so hardcore..."

"Hardcore?" No one had ever called me that before. *What, as in hardcore boob-toucher? Now that's a rep I don't think I want.*

"Uhhh...sorry, but I think I'm gonna have to decline," she continued, waving a dismissive hand. Alas, no Didney Worl for me.

"Yeah, no, that's totally fine. If Adachi found out I touched them, she'd kill both of us." *In fact, she might already kill me just for talking to you.* "She can get kinda jelly sometimes."

Honestly, *kinda* was an understatement. I was practically her entire world. We weren't just "lovey-dovey"—more like lovey-lovey-lovey-lovey-lovey-lovey-lovey-dovey.

"Wow. I never would have guessed at first glance...but then again, I can see it." Panchos smiled wistfully like she'd thought of something, and it made me curious.

"Oh, yeah? How so?"

"Whenever she looks at something, she has tunnel vision. Nothing else matters."

Whoa, she's been paying attention. Secretly, I was impressed.

"Personally, I prefer strawberry jelly," said my backpack. I gave it a hard smack.

"Huh?" Panchos glanced around, but I pretended not to notice her confusion. "Eh, I guess a building this old's bound to have a ghost or two," she concluded after a moment.

It's alarming how readily you shrug things off, but in this case, I appreciate it.

"Anyway, not to get too far into sexual territory, but I wanted to ask you..."

"Uh, I think we're already past that point..."

She cleared her throat, and I braced myself for whatever she was about to ask me next. That way I could be prepared for it without getting flustered. Then, in a low voice, she asked: "Have you ever seen Adachi-san naked?"

"Yeah, yesterday."

"*Yesterday*?!"

She hit the back of her head against the wall in shock, but it didn't seem to hurt. *Her head must be pretty buff... Wait, how does that work?* If she ran around bashing her skull on things, it would probably crack.

"Oh, wait, you mean in the hot spring?" she eventually realized.

"Yeah, where else?"

"I mean…" She faltered, blushing pink, then blurted hastily, "Like, when you're alone in a room together?! You know what I mean, right?!"

"Right."

"*Right*?!" she repeated like a parrot. Then, once she was calm, she thought of another question: "So who made the first move?"

"Adachi." Quietly, I scoffed at myself for answering all her questions so easily.

"I knew it!" She snickered, and I found myself feeling a little indignant.

"Did you, now?"

"Well, you don't really seem interested in other people," she explained offhandedly, inadvertently jabbing at my sore spot. "You make an effort to be nice, but on the inside, I get the feeling you don't actually care."

As I fell silent, however, she cheerfully continued.

"Actually, let me back up. It's not that you don't *care*—it's kinda related to the thing I mentioned about the clothes you wear on a date, I guess? I don't mean this in a bad way, but…you're just not ambitious. You accept things the way they already are."

I found myself listening with rapt attention. I had barely

spoken to this girl, and yet she seemed to know me inside and out... Her powers of observation were downright frightening. Or were Adachi and I just that easy to read?

"Is it the way I act or something?"

"In the past, yeah. But lately you've stopped."

"Well, how do I act now?"

"Now? Like a lovey steady girlfriend, natch."

Wait, what happened to dovey? For that matter, if everyone else saw me as some dutiful girlfriend, then what did Adachi have to complain about?

"It's always *lovey this, lovey that* with you, isn't it?"

"Oh, Shimamura-san. I bet you're seeing the world through lovey-colored glasses right this very moment."

"That sounds terrifying."

What color would that be? Red? Adachi's definitely red a lot of the time. Mostly her cheeks and ears. And she even sprayed red when she confessed her love to me.

"Knowing what sort of girl you are, the fact that you choose to be with Adachi-san is proof of just how much you've come to care about her," Panchos remarked casually.

Wait, what?

Her tone was so light and easygoing, it made the words themselves hit that much harder, like a ray of light shining into the depths of a sea cave. Or maybe it only resonated with me because I'd let my guard down at that exact moment. Whatever it was, it shone brighter than the hallway lights overhead.

"...I think I understand."

Maybe she was right; maybe Adachi *was* special to me. *Hmmmm...* Despite my emotional reaction, however, Panchos carried on freely.

"Let me know if your lovey-dovey energy starts to run low and I'll steal the girls away so you can have some private time... Oh, but then again, I'm not sure I could sleep in the same room knowing *certain things* took place in there...!" she muttered to herself.

"I appreciate the thought, but I think I'll pass."

I didn't want to make this school trip any more complicated than it already was. Besides, sooner or later we'd—*we'd what?* I tried to examine this passing thought in greater detail, but it slipped away like sand through my fingers. When I tried to force myself to remember, I could feel my brain starting to cramp up.

"Anyway, you don't have to worry about the rest of us. You two should go do your own thing."

"At least that way we won't make you guys feel awkward, either, right?"

"True," she admitted readily, and I appreciated her honesty. Then she pulled away from the wall. "Welp, thanks for talking to me. It was fun!"

Likewise, I didn't get to have this kind of conversation every day, and I enjoyed it. All that remained was to pray Panchos would keep her mouth shut. *I hope her lips are as toned as her biceps.*

"The most important thing I learned from this is that you're even more fun than I thought you were. See you later, Shimamura-san!"

As she walked off, the flattened heels of her shoes made a funny sound...and as it faded away into the distance, I realized I was holding my breath. I exhaled and felt my headache ease slightly. The two of us had talked for so long that if this were a horror movie, we both would have died. Fortunately, we kept things casual, or else Adachi herself might have stabbed us.

"Want some tea?" I asked my backpack. A single pale hand shot out of it. *Eegh.* "Stick your head out, too, please."

"Whoosh!" The mysterious life-form heeded my request, and so I handed her the bottle of light barley tea. "Slurp, slurp!"

Spare me the sound effects, please.

"It appears you're having a rather difficult time, aren't you, Shimamura-san?"

"So it appears."

"Then I shall go to sleep."

"Sweet dreams."

A moment later, I could hear the sounds of muffled snoring. *Man, I wish my life were as simple as yours.* I slung my backpack over my shoulder and headed back to our assigned room, belatedly following after Panchos. She must have known I'd show up, too, because the door was ajar.

When I stepped inside, three of the five were still curled up under their blankets. As for Panchos, she had opened the curtains and was now peering out at the surrounding forest beneath the morning rays. The deep green hue was still dim from the last vestiges of night. As I gazed out at it, I could practically smell the rich earthy fragrance.

Adachi began to squirm, as if in protest of the light. I crouched down beside her and gave her a little shake. She must have been mostly awake already, because her eyes snapped open.

"Morning!" I greeted her.

She blinked at me in alarm—probably surprised that I,

notorious sloth that I am, actually woke up ahead of her. Or was she still sensitive about what happened in the hot spring last night? Slowly but surely, her eyes focused.

"Good morning, Shimamura." The next thing I knew, she was gazing down sadly at her empty left hand.

Meanwhile, I could see Panchos out of the corner of my eye, nodding with her arms folded. I didn't know what exactly she was approving of, but it made me laugh.

On day two of the trip, we would be taking the bus to a theme park...according to the itinerary, at least. After breakfast, we were instructed to pack up and gather out front, suggesting there wasn't much leeway in the schedule today. The buses were already on their way here.

Outside, the mountains seemed to block out all sunlight, and the morning air was crisp and cold. Like yesterday, the sky was clear, with few clouds to speak of. But today the buses had a little detour to make before we reached our destination.

"This theme park's supposed to look like the Netherlands. What does 'Netherlands' bring to mind for you?" I asked Adachi sitting next to me.

"Nothing," she replied brusquely, shaking her head. Then, after a moment, her cheeks flushed pink, and she hastily turned her head away in the direction of the window.

"I'll go ahead and refrain from asking what it was you just thought of..."

"It...it's nothing!"

"Uh oh! The girl from Planet Nothing is back!" I teased, and in the window's reflection, I could see her pouting her lips.

Outside, the road was growing increasingly narrow, steep, and windy. Evidently, we were traveling from one mountain to another. *Ugh, boring. I see enough mountains back home,* I thought to myself. Nonetheless, I couldn't take my eyes off the scenery.

In my mind, the conversation with Panchos kept flickering to life. To me, it seemed like a meaningful moment, and yet what I remembered most were the stupid parts, like *Hoohoo, hottie.* Internally, I rolled my eyes at myself. Then, at long last, my gaze drifted to the subject of that discussion: Adachi. I took in her face in profile, her colors faint and muted like the first day of autumn.

I was fond of her—that much I could say for sure. I let her get away with things that I'd never tolerate from someone I didn't know as well. Thus, I wasn't opposed to spending time with her. So how far could we go together? And how long was I expecting it to last? As of this moment, the answer to the first was: to the edge of the country. As for the second...it remained to be seen.

The long, long bus ride carried us to the foot of a different mountain. I knew its name, and I knew it was an active volcano. But instead of actually taking us up that mountain, we were brought instead to a spacious parking lot. The teachers explained that we would be making a stop here.

All around me, I could feel the other students silently asking the same question: *Is this our destination? A parking lot?* But the riddle was solved once we made it about halfway in. The entire area was blanketed with fog so thick, it felt like we'd driven straight into a cloud.

"I can't see anything," Adachi muttered, her face pressed against the window pane. Likewise, other students were doing the same. We didn't *ever* get fog this thick back home.

Then the teachers instructed us to exit the bus and experience the fog on foot. As a precaution, they warned us to stay near the bus, though I wasn't confident anyone was actually going to listen. I debated whether to leave my backpack on my seat, but ultimately, I decided to bring it along. No real reason, other than I figured Yashiro might enjoy the fog.

And so we all poured out of the bus, my fear and curiosity piqued by the shrieks elicited from the people ahead of me. I looked over my shoulder and saw Adachi behind me, looking generally unimpressed...and then it was my turn.

"This is nuts..."

The instant I stepped down onto the pavement, I could no longer see a thing. Or, more accurately, the only thing I could see was the thick white fog. By the time I turned back, the entire bus had disappeared.

All around me, I could hear my classmates squealing in delight, but I couldn't parse the distance between us, and it was starting to confuse me. I shivered. It was colder here than back at the hot spring inn.

"So this is what it means to be mist-ified... Wait, no, that's *mystified* with a Y," I corrected myself aloud. It still felt like it fit, though. Surrounded by walls of white on all sides, I was at a total loss.

Just then, someone's disembodied shoulder popped out from the fog, and I flinched in surprise. I could only see about a foot in front of my own face. One wrong step and someone might actually get lost out here.

But then a realization dawned on me, and far too late:

In my excitement to experience the fog, I had already taken quite a few steps away from the bus. I thought Adachi was right behind me, but when I looked over my shoulder, I couldn't see her. At this point, I wasn't even sure I was facing the bus.

"Shimamura!"

In the fog, I could hear Adachi calling for me. "Adachi!" I called back.

"Shimamura! Shimamura!"

But without any visual landmarks, I couldn't tell which direction the voice was coming from. Before now, I never knew my hearing was linked to my sight at all. The lack of sensory information was starting to drive me crazy.

"Where are you?"

"Over here!"

If we were both actively searching for each other, it would only make it harder to actually *find* each other. That much was plain to see, and yet I knew Adachi wouldn't stop. *Guess it's up to me, then.* As I stood still, I could hear the teachers calling the students back to the bus, but couldn't tell where they were. Part of me wondered why they would send us out into this fog in the first place, but on second thought, they probably didn't realize what they were in for either.

Either way, the fog didn't stretch on endlessly. Worst-case scenario, as long as I stayed put, someone would surely find me sooner or later. Luckily for me, I wasn't the restless type. Adjusting my backpack straps, I faced forward and listened for the faint sounds of Adachi's voice. The white walls filled my vision.

This was my world without Adachi: hazy, impenetrable, nothing worth an ounce of energy. In a way, it reminded me of my lazy days as a high school first-year. *No wonder I always felt so trapped,* I thought to myself. But now, I was in a very different place, and when I thought about the reason why, my legs started to move on autopilot. Suddenly, I was *desperate* to find Adachi.

Somehow, my backpack sensed this about me. "On your right."

My right? Per Yashiro's instructions, I reached out with my right hand, and as the icy mist seemed to drain all warmth from my fingers...I brushed against what felt like a shoulder. Someone was next to me, right there in the fog. The other person flinched, tentatively touched my fingers—then, with renewed certainty, grabbed my entire hand. Honestly, who needed sight when I could recognize that vise grip anywhere?

"Shimamura! I found you!"

Adachi came walking out from behind the fog, grasping my hand in both of hers. There was something reassuring in the way she held me so tightly... We were only apart for less than a minute total, but now that we were together again, I had never been more thrilled to see her. Likewise, she was beaming from ear to ear in a rare display of glee.

So we stood there holding hands, the same way we did last night, except this time, the fog was here to keep us hidden.

"Thank you," I whispered quietly, not to Adachi, but to my backpack.

"I shall go back to sleep now."

"Okay, okay."

Her snores sounded like something out of an anime; they mingled with the distant sounds of birds chirping.

"Who are you talking to?"

"Oh, just myself, as usual. Anyways...man, this is crazy, huh? Not to sound like a broken record or anything."

Adachi was literally right next to me, and yet her face had already disappeared back into the fog; all I could see now was our joined hands. Was she still smiling? Either way, with a landmark now on my right, I already had a better sense of my surroundings. Our hands served as a signpost for both of us.

"Wanna walk around a little?"

I knew the teachers wanted us to head back to the bus, but I felt like exploring. Now that I had accomplished my goal of finding Adachi, I had no set destination in mind. The two of us could go anywhere.

"You may have forgotten, but I'm actually a delinquent. A bad girl." And with our hands linked, I had surely rubbed off on her. Hence, I extended this rebellious invitation.

I still couldn't see her face, but I could feel her answer from the way her hand shifted against mine. "Let's do it."

"Cool."

"This is probably the only chance I'll get to walk hand in hand with you."

At first I didn't understand what she meant, but then I realized she was referring to the fog obscuring us from sight. *Gotcha.* "Wow, Adachi, I didn't realize you were self-conscious about this stuff."

"...Not really. But I know *you* are, so..."

It felt like an eternity since the last time she made an effort to be this considerate. Did the hot spring improve her blood pressure and restore her mental composure? If so, then my shameless nudity had paid off.

Ahem. All jokes aside.

"You're not much of a bad girl at all, are you?"

I thought I had corrupted her, but instead, I was basically absconding with her. *Eh, good enough,* I thought, and started walking. Was there any point to us doing this? Yes. I was trying to give my heart what it wanted. Nothing could possibly be more important. I just wanted to walk through the fog.

Adachi and I walked straight forward. There was a path ahead of us. Even if other people couldn't see it, it was still there.

"When I lost you in the fog, I thought..."

"Hmm?"

Her fingers tightened around mine, pulling me closer. "I thought to myself, *This is probably what my life would be like without her.*"

Without my sense of sight, I couldn't see her face... but instead, it felt like I could see straight through to her heart. Or was she always such an open book?

"...Shimamura?"

I debated whether or not I should say it, but since my face was safely hidden, I decided to go for it. "Me too."

"...Huh?!"

"I thought the same thing."

I giggled awkwardly. Then, she yanked hard on my arm like she was ringing a church bell. "Repeat that?!"

"Sorry, no can do. The fog's clearing up." And if I had to look her in the eye while I said it, I would probably die of embarrassment.

"It's not clearing up at all, though!"

"Sure it is! The more we breathe it in, the more it disappears," I explained like a total imbecile as we walked straight ahead.

It felt like we were taking small steps toward our future waiting just on the horizon, though we couldn't quite see it. It reminded me of the view from the boat—looking out across the water, with absolutely nothing else in sight—and yet, in both cases, I felt no fear, regardless of what I could or couldn't see. As long as the two of us were together, nothing could mist-ify me. For the first time in my life, I felt invincible.

After that, we filed back onto the bus and headed to the theme park, as planned. Then Adachi and I ditched our assigned group and slipped away to a place where flowers filled every last crevice. But ultimately, nothing left a stronger impact than the moment in the fog that day.

On the second night, we stayed at a hotel—a much taller building than the hot spring inn. When I looked up at it, its overall shape reminded me of a slice of castella cake. Honest, that was my first impression. But when I told Adachi, she called me a weirdo.

No hotel room was big enough to fit five people, so each group was split into two. Naturally, the second Panchos found out about this, she immediately stepped into the role of wingwoman: "The three of us will sleep in this room, so you two can have fun in the other!"

It was *sooo* extremely obvious what she was doing, but the rest of the Trio let her drag them off without any objection. Not like any of them would have much fun sharing a room with me and Adachi. And Yashiro too, but nobody else knew she was here, so she kinda didn't count.

I set my backpack down at the edge of my bed, plopped down onto it, and let out a breath. "My feet hurt," I announced, summing up my thoughts about today in a single statement. There was still an hour left until dinnertime, and if I lay down, I could fill it in a blink. In fact, I could probably nap for a good three hours or so.

Resisting the temptation to curl up into a toasty little ball, I noticed Adachi sitting on the bed next to mine, fidgeting. She was practically hunched over in a kneeling position.

"Is something wrong?" I asked her.

"Just thinking...we're alone now," she remarked timidly. Was it really that noteworthy?

"Aren't we usually alone whenever we hang out at my house and stuff?" For that matter, we'd been spending time alone since we first met in the gym loft.

"Yeahbutthisisahotel," she muttered in a single breath, staring up at the ceiling.

Oh, right. I get it. "Oh, no, my womanly virtue!"

"Wha?!"

"Heeeelp!" As a joke, I covered the areas of my body that she'd paid the most attention to back in the hot spring (use your imagination). But then again, she was staring so fervently that she might have developed x-ray vision...or, in plainer terms, already memorized every detail.

She realized what I was suggesting and her eyes widened. "Nottrueit'snothing!" she spluttered.

"Setting aside what exactly is 'not true' and 'nothing,' which I will be sure to follow up on at a later date..." I kicked my shoes off, flopped down, and curled into a ball on the left side of the bed. Then I reached out in her direction. "Care to join me?"

A beat later, she recoiled sharply. "Wh-what about your womanly virtue?!"

"Relax. I trust you."

At no point was I actually worried that she was going to cross any boundaries. After all this time together, I had obviously learned where her limits were. But of course, that didn't stop her from acting in unpredictable ways.

"I thought you might like it if we cuddled."

Besides, it was silly to shout across the room at each other from separate beds. The longer it took for her words to reach me, the more likely I might doze off. Heck, I was already starting to yawn. I needed Adachi to keep me tethered to the waking world.

"Anyway, open invitation, if you're interested."

"Uhh...okay...thank you."

She shuffled over and perched at the very edge of my bed. Then she hastily threw herself down onto her side, smashing her face into my shoulder. Hard.

"Ow!"

The impact was enough to leave a big red mark on her forehead, so as you might expect, it was painful for me too. Then she gazed silently into my eyes, our noses practically touching. Giggling bashfully, I greeted her with a smile. "Welcome."

"Uh…hi."

I loved her faltering little pauses. From here, the next thing she would want was probably…

"Wanna put your head on my arm? Or mine on yours?"

I gave my arm a little wiggle. She gazed at it hesitantly, and then…

"What about both?"

"Oooh, good idea."

We each slid an arm under the other's head. Admittedly it was kind of an awkward position, but this way we could both enjoy the weight against our own arm and the pillowy softness of the other's. I guess we could have simply taken turns, but that wasn't a very elegant solution.

As she rested against me, her hair tickled my skin.

"So how did you like your school trip?" I asked, almost like I was her mother. But that was a recurring element in my relationship with her.

Man, I'm too young to be a mom. I kept hoping there was some way I could stay a "big sister" type at most. Now *that*, I was already good at.

"…Pretty average, I think," she replied flatly. As someone who wasn't comfortable in group settings, there was simply no way she was going to enjoy this type of event.

"Well, did you like the hot spring, at least?"

"Wh...?! You...you ditz! No, I mean...you bully!"

That first one felt a little harsh. Then she started flailing the arm under my head, smacking me.

"I was joking! I mean, I'd say it's pretty average for me too." Sure, I was having fun and making new discoveries, but... "It's like when my parents bring me somewhere, you know?"

Because I didn't pay for that plane ticket with my own money. For now, this was as far as I could go.

As we lay on the bed, my eyes wandered to the upside-down scenery. Through the open curtains, I could see a cloudless night sky. "So here's something I learned earlier today: the morning after a cloudless night is more likely to be foggy."

"Huh."

"I guess you never know what tomorrow might bring, huh?"

The day before I met Adachi, I had no idea she was about to become a part of my life. Now here she was, cuddling in bed with me. Who could have seen this coming? The future was a mystery enshrouded in fog.

"See, I'm actually kinda curious to find out just how far we can go together," I explained, gazing at her with my head tilted sideways. Adachi didn't react strongly to this, probably because I hadn't explained my thought process, so I continued. "For now, we still need adults to take us everywhere, but what about in five or ten years? Where will we be then? Right now, I haven't the *foggiest* idea, but I'd like to take steps toward it."

Walking blindly through the darkness, I had no confidence that I was actually moving forward. But as long as Adachi was around to hold my hand, the two of us would surely find our way.

She looked at me, her eyes unblinking and as round as saucers. "Uh, I don't think I totally understand," she replied in a breathy voice.

"Eh, I didn't expect you to."

Her arm quivered under my head. "But...setting that aside..."

Hey, c'mon, don't just cast it aside!

"Are you saying...you'll still want to be with me in ten years...?" she asked shyly, hoping to confirm the part that, to her, was the most important.

Ten years... Part of me was worried that I was overpromising, but at the same time, I wanted her to know how I was feeling right now. "I'd like to be."

I'd never taken anything as seriously as I took Adachi. And likewise, Adachi only ever seemed to think about me.

This was enough to make it work with just the two of us. At the very least, it gave me a casual landmark to strive toward.

Adachi's eyes widened, gleaming with joy. It was the same expression I'd seen on her face when she saw her name on the class list at the start of the school year.

"It'll take at least ten years, but...would you wanna travel abroad with me?"

But as I revisited the same promise I had previously declined, a different girl's face rose to mind... We'd need to have an important conversation after we got home.

"Wait, so when you said 'how far we can go,' you meant, like...literally?"

"Uh, yeah...?" Traveling long distances required time, money, and a lot of preparation. I was inviting her to share it with me.

Adachi shook her head vigorously, whipping at my arm with her hair—but in a way, the sting was comforting.

"Tomorrow's still too foggy."

"...Okay, then." I didn't mind the fog, since we could always hold hands again.

And so the veil of night descended on our little trip. For us, it was our first, but it also marked the promise of many more to come.

Many hours later...

"I'm hoooome!"

"Welcome back. Where's my luxury souvenir?"

"Right, your souvenir... How about you open my backpack over there?"

My luggage entered the house ahead of me. My sister raced over to it, but before she could open it, it opened itself, and the souvenir peeked her head out.

"Oh, it's Yachi!"

Immediately followed by a bizarre *slrrrp* sound.

4. Headed Home

"**T**HE PLANE ENGINES always sound like they're working hard to carry us, y'know?" Shimamura remarked as we traveled through the airport. "When I hear that *VRRRRNNN*, I feel like I'm cargo." Her hands floated unsteadily through the air, mimicking liftoff.

"Uhhhh...okay." Personally, I never stopped to think about that while I was on the plane; I just kinda zoned out. And since I didn't know what it felt like to be cargo, I couldn't relate to her analogy. "So you like the sound of the engines?"

"Mmm, not really. Too loud," she shrugged offhandedly. Classic Shimamura—first, she made it sound like she enjoyed it, and now this. She was a total ditz, but I loved that about her.

Unlike the last time we were here, my pace was hasty. *Checkout isn't for a few more hours*, or *it's not that far from the hotel*, or *we won't get another chance for who knows how long*—bit by bit, I had let her convince me we still had time. We probably should have gone to see that famous crab wheel yesterday instead. But at the same time, there was meaning in going to see it today...according to Shimamura, anyway.

Now the trip was over, and we were on our way home. All that remained was to get on the plane and fly back to Japan. But Shimamura was blatantly unmotivated, in part because her over-packed luggage was so heavy. Plus, she generally wasn't too good at organizational tasks. She didn't seem to ever want to *finish* anything...but I was planning to stick around for as long as it took her.

To sum it up: The trip was really fun. Shimamura was with me, so I enjoyed it. But the fun of it was built on a foundation that would take a long time to actually explain. We dreamed of going somewhere far away together, and then that dream came true, and it felt like a dream the whole time. But unlike any other dream, I never wanted to forget it.

For now, it was still too early to look back and reflect on it. Knowing me, I'd probably relive these moments over and over—whenever I raised my head, whenever I saw my souvenirs, every night when I went to sleep. Was there anything more important to have gained on this trip than the memories we created?

"Oh, wait a sec!"

Despite the rush I was in, Shimamura remained un-hurried. At one point, she spotted a little souvenir kiosk and made a detour, so I decided to take a peek with her. As we walked around looking at the shelves, the refresh-ing scent of chocolate filled the air; it must've been this smell that reminded her of something she'd forgotten, because she promptly bought some.

"I should have expected they wouldn't have any famous jam buns here," she muttered to herself. Then I realized just who this souvenir was for and scowled.

To me, the affection she showed that mysterious life-form was slightly different from that which she showed me and everyone else, and at one point in my life, I re-sented it. In fact, to this day, I hadn't fully gotten over it. As she walked away from the souvenir kiosk, I called out to her.

"Hey, Shimamura?"

"What's up?"

"I'd like it if you'd buy me a souvenir too."

"Uhhhh..." Her eyes shifted through all the different lunar phases, widening and narrowing. "But...you're here with me now..."

"I know." *Is that a song lyric or something?*

"Er, forgive me, my dear Adachi, but I'm afraid I don't understand," she replied with the cadence of a butler. *"I'm sorry,"* she tacked on in English.

Where was this bilingual proficiency back on the plane to California? It's too late now!

"I mean...as a memento of the trip?"

"...Okay...?" The look on her face suggested she still didn't get it. Nevertheless, she sprang to action. "Let'sh shee here..." Muttering under her breath, she scanned the shelves once more. Spotting something cute, she stared at it for a good five seconds before picking it up and buying it on the spot. "Here's your souvenir!"

She had chosen...a ceramic cup, warm yellow-green in color. When I took it, I noticed the price tag was still stuck to the bottom.

"Why this?"

"Well, you like water."

"...True...?"

"So there you go."

I still couldn't see how those two statements were

related. "Why do these souvenir shops always have a bunch of ceramics, anyway?"

"I dunno… If they're so common, then maybe they have a strong pottery industry."

"Isn't that more of a Japan thing?"

She tapped her temple knowingly, and I rolled my eyes. *As if you know a single thing about this country.* Dubiously, I held the cup up to the light in the distance. Would anyone in Japan believe me if I told them it was American-made?

"…Oh, well," I muttered as I viewed the world through a yellow-green lens. Now I was starting to sound like Shimamura.

I didn't really care what she gave me—whether it came from across the Pacific or just the local supermarket. She always gave me what I needed, no matter how selfish, and always with a smile. This alone hadn't changed since the first day I met her, and now it was the signpost that guided me through life.

"Weird how going home is always such a relief, huh?" Shimamura commented with a grin once we had settled into our seats on the plane.

I could kinda see where she was coming from. But for her, "home" was two different places... It made me both a little jealous and a little sad too.

Later, during the flight, I thought back over what she said earlier. Before now, the sound of the plane engines was only a nuisance, but suddenly, I found myself focusing on it ever so slightly. When I raised my head to listen to it, it was just noise. So instead, I closed my eyes and pretended to be Shimamura's cargo.

Before I knew it, my imagination was flying faster than the plane.

As if retracing our steps, we passed through customs and left the airport. The fatigue that plagued us was proof of the time we'd spent in a far-off land.

"Hey, Shimamura?"

I could tell I was home from the humidity in the air. We had traveled a long way to get back here, and now another dull chore awaited us: unpacking. Regardless, I decided to carry on like we were still on vacation. I didn't know how long it would last, but once it petered out...

"Let's go again sometime," I remarked as I looked over my shoulder at the airport terminal.

Beside me, I saw Shimamura follow my gaze. "Sure, once we save up enough."

"Cool."

At some point along the line, we had learned how to give each other soft, airy dreams to pad out the cold, hard reality. And personally, I really liked the relationship we'd built together.

That was my overall review of the past ten years with Shimamura.

Afterword

AND THERE YOU HAVE IT: the end of *Adachi and Shimamura* Volume 8. Did you miss me? Yes, hello. Apologies for the long wait.

This volume opens with a story set in the future, basically a "final episode" sort of thing, but this is *not* the final volume. See, I figured out how I wanted *Adachi and Shimamura* to end, so I decided to go ahead and write it now. This way, the series will have a conclusive ending, in the event that I spontaneously die in a fit of rage or something.

Incidentally, I have no plans to die at this time. Imagine if I did, though. That would be frightening.

I mean, I *am* going to die someday, obviously. We all do in the end. This is something we tend to forget when we're busy living peaceful lives. But hey, I'd rather spend my days having fun. I figure I'll worry about kicking the bucket whenever I arrive at the bucket.

Anyway, *Adachi and Shimamura* is going to continue for a little longer. And in fact, there's going to be a big announcement soon... Well, by the time you read this, I expect it's already been announced. But as of this writing, I still have no idea, so I hope you'll all be excited.

Once again, thank you very much. Oh, yeah, and feel free to pick up *Regarding Saeki Sayaka* as well.

—Hitoma Iruma